To Annie and San

CARLA CASSIDY

is the author of ten young-adult novels, as well as her many contemporary romances. She's been a cheerleader for the Kansas City Chiefs football team and has travelled the East Coast as a singer and dancer in a band, but the greatest pleasure she's had is in creating romance and happiness for readers.

Chapter One

Abby Jones jumped out of the car at the red light and slammed the door. "Creep," she muttered beneath her breath, shoving a strand of the blond wig out of her eyes.

Looking both ways, she quickly got off the road and up onto the sidewalk, her footsteps quick and angry.

This was the last time, the very last time she let her daughter fix her up on a blind date. Charlene was a devoted, wonderful daughter, but as a matchmaker, the fourteen-year-old definitely missed her mark.

I'll ground her for a week, Abby thought, unable to believe her daughter had managed to talk her into going out with Walter Simmons, the man she'd just escaped from at the stoplight. It was easy to understand why Walter was so successful as a member of the wind section of the Baldwin Philharmonic Orchestra. The man was full of hot air. Worse than that, they'd attended a charity costume party. Walt had come dressed as a vampire, then had spent the rest of the evening trying to suck on her neck.

I'll ground her for a month, she amended, looking around to get her bearings. Spying a phone booth on the next corner, she dug in the bottom of her purse to find a quarter. At least she'd chosen to jump ship at a place where a phone was nearby. Now all she had to do was call one of her friends to come and get her.

She went into the phone booth, deposited her money and quickly punched in seven numbers. As she waited for the connection to go through, her gaze swept up and down the street. Of all the places in town, why had she picked this particular seedy intersection to say au revoir to her date? She smiled wryly. Because it was at this particular intersection that Walt had transformed himself from a vampire to a wolf, pawing and groping at her with what seemed to be eight hands. She shuddered at the memory of his clammy touch and hot breath.

As she looked once again out the booth windows, she suppressed another shudder. Baldwin, Indiana was a nice city, but like all mid-size cities there were areas where sane, normal people didn't venture after dark. And this was definitely one of those areas.

"Come on, come on," she muttered impatiently, hoping her sister was home to receive the call. After several unanswered rings, she hung up. She retrieved her quarter, deposited it again and punched in seven new numbers. Surely one of her friends would be home on a Saturday night.

As she waited impatiently for the connection to go through, she noticed flashing red lights signaling the approach of an emergency vehicle. She grimaced, realizing such a sight was probably commonplace in this part of town.

As she watched, a paddy wagon pulled up next to the curb. She hung up the telephone, realizing her friend Kathy apparently wasn't home, either. Didn't anyone stay home on Saturday nights anymore?

For the third time she dropped in her quarter, irritably punching in another set of numbers. She whirled around as the door of the booth flew open. She sighed in relief as she came face-to-face with a young police officer.

"Okay, sweetheart, hang up the phone. That's one date you won't be keeping."

"I beg your pardon?" Abby looked at him in confusion.

"I said hang up the phone." She did as he requested, gasping in surprise as he took her arm and pulled her out of the phone booth. "Come on, honey. It's roundup night. The mayor wants all you working girls off the streets."

"Working girls?" Abby stopped in her tracks and stared at him, a nervous bubble of laughter escaping her lips. "Oh no, you can't think that I..." But, of course he could, she thought fatalistically. Here she stood before him, clad in a frowsy blond wig, a black leather miniskirt, metallic strapless blouse and enough makeup to make Mae West look like a natural beauty.

It had been Charlene's idea that she dress up like a punk rocker. *I'll ground her for a year,* Abby decided. "Look," she began, giving the officer a hesitant smile. "This is all a terrible misunderstanding. I'm not a...a...hooker. I've been to a costume party and I had a fight with my date—" She broke off at the officer's look of disbelief. "Really, this is all a horrible mistake."

"Honey, the only mistake you made was working the streets on a roundup night." He took her arm once again and led her toward the waiting paddy wagon.

Abby pulled her arm away from his grasp. "Please, listen to me...this is a misunderstanding."

The officer sighed wearily. "Lady, just get in the wagon before I lose my patience and add resisting arrest to your charges. You can discuss this 'misunderstanding' with the judge."

"The judge!" Abby started to protest again, but one look at the policeman's expression told her she'd better do as he asked. She stepped up into the back of the paddy wagon already occupied by several other women. She sat down on the bench inside, feeling like she'd suddenly climbed into a bad dream.

"This is a nightmare," she breathed aloud as the back door of the wagon was slammed shut and locked. "This can't be happening."

"First bust?" Abby looked at the young woman next to her. Actually, she was little more than a teenager, but her eyes looked old, world-weary. "First bust?" she repeated.

"Yes... I mean... no... I mean this is all a big mistake." Abby flushed, realizing her statement had managed to garner the attention of all the other women. "You see, I was on my way home from a costume party, a charity affair for the Philharmonic. My date was a real creep so I got out of his car and was making a phone call when the policeman just assumed..." She looked at all the women. "It was all just a crazy mistake."

"I know what you mean." A red-haired woman in a purple negligee nodded. "I was just on my way back to the convent when those mean cops nabbed me." Her words brought hoots of laughter and catcalls from the other women.

"Yeah, and I was on my way to the hospital to visit my poor sick mother," another one said, flipping a strand of her gold-streaked hair behind her shoulder.

"No, you don't understand. I'm really a teacher," Abby protested. "I teach high school and for extra money I teach adult education." She knew she was rambling, but the unreality of the situation was making her nervous.

"Yeah, I'm a teacher, too," one of the others snickered. "But you can't find what I teach in no textbook." Again the wagon filled with raucous laughter, and Abby decided it would be best if she just kept her mouth shut until they got to the police station and she could get this mess cleared up.

The ride to the station seemed interminable. Abby listened to the conversation going on around her, noting how the women bandied about the names of prosecuting attorneys and judges as if they were personal friends. None of the women seemed particularly nervous or upset; there was more of a party atmosphere.

"Don't worry," the young girl next to Abby spoke again as they were being led into the police station. "It's really no big deal. All they can book most of us on is loitering or disturbing the peace. You just plead guilty, pay the fine and you should be out of here within a couple of hours."

"I'm not going to plead guilty," Abby protested indignantly. "I'm not guilty."

The young girl eyed Abby with a wry grin. "Yeah, right, we're all not guilty. We're just all misunderstood."

There was no more time for small talk as everyone was led into a room where forms were filled out and fingerprints taken. After being booked, they were locked in a holding tank where Abby did her best not to panic.

The other prisoners acted as if it was old home week, talking about favorite dates and going into details that made Abby's ears turn red. Thankfully she was in there only a few minutes before an officer came to let her make the phone call she'd been requesting since the moment she'd entered the station.

She immediately called her friend and lawyer, Harry Meeker.

"Harry, it's Abby," she said in relief when he answered the phone. "I have a small problem and could use your help. I've been arrested and need you here for legal advice." There was a long, pregnant pause at the other end of the line. "Harry?"

"Abby, hon, you won't believe what I just thought you said."

"You heard me right, Harry. Please, please come down here and get me out of this. I'm at the Third Precinct."

"I'll be there in fifteen minutes."

It was nearly an hour later when Abby was once again led out of the cell and taken to a hallway outside the courtroom where night court was taking place.

"Oh my gawd." Harry hurried toward her, his pinched little face radiating amusement. "Abby, love, what have you done to yourself?" He reached up and touched one of her platinum curls. "I love the color, but the style does nothing for you."

Abby glared at the little man. "Cut the crap, Harry. I've had a bad night."

"Darling, you've absolutely made my night." Harry laughed then sobered as she shot him another scathing glare. "My, we *have* had a bad night, haven't we?"

"Harry, tonight I suffered through the blind date from hell, thanks to my dear daughter. That experience could only have been topped by being arrested for prostitution and thrown into a jail cell where I learned more about sex than I ever wanted to ask."

Harry grinned, started to say something, then pulled her over to a bench and sat her down. "Don't worry, I'll take care of this. They're going to call your case in just a few minutes. Tell me what happened."

As quickly as possible, Abby told him the events of the evening, from the moment she'd jumped out of Walt's car, to the present.

When she was finished he patted her hand. "Don't worry. I'm sure this can be worked out quite easily. I'll just explain the situation to the judge and chances are he'll dismiss the whole thing."

She nodded, and together, along with an accompanying officer, they entered the courtroom.

Abby hadn't been in a courtroom since the day of her divorce ten years before. That particular proceeding had been held in the middle of a Tuesday afternoon and the room had been packed. At one o'clock on a Sunday morning, the room was almost empty save for the accused awaiting their turn to speak to the judge.

"Oh, great," Harry murmured beneath his breath as they slid onto a bench at the back of the courtroom.

"What's wrong?" Abby asked anxiously, seeing the frown on Harry's face.

He motioned to the judge at the front of the courtroom. "That's the esteemed Judge Eldridge Stewart...Stoneface Stewart, as we in the legal system like to call him. Of course, we don't call him that to his face. The man has no sense of humor."

Abby looked at the judge with interest. He seemed relatively young to be in such an exalted position. His dark hair was thick and just beginning to gray at the temples. His features were finely tooled, chiseled by a force that combined beauty with strength. The arrogant straightness of his nose, the firm jawline broken only by the hint of a cleft in the chin—yes, it was a face of great character and strength. But it was his eyes that struck her. There was no mercy in their gray depths, no compassion, only a blank coldness that made a shiver race up her spine.

"He looks mean," she whispered to Harry.

Harry grimaced. "If this were the Old West, Judge Stewart would be the equivalent of a hanging judge. He's a hard man."

Abby rubbed her forehead with the tip of two fingers where a major headache was beginning to blossom with nauseating intensity. "Just get me out of here. I have a daughter to kill."

Harry laughed. "Keep in mind, if you follow through on that particular thought, you'll end up right back in here facing Judge Stewart."

Within minutes Abby's name was called and she found herself standing in front of the "hanging judge," his cold eyes glaring at her as if she were dirt he'd dug out from beneath his fingernails.

Abby flushed beneath his intense stare as Harry began to tell him the circumstances of her presence in court.

"So you see, Your Honor," Harry concluded, "my client is a hard-working, upstanding single parent whose only crime is having an exceptionally abhorrent blind date."

This last statement made Abby glare at Harry once again. He didn't have to tell the judge that, for goodness' sake!

Those cold gray eyes stared at her long and hard. "I suggest, Mrs. Jones, that you be more selective in your dating habits in the future," he said, his voice ringing with undisputed authority. His gaze held hers for a moment longer. "Case dismissed." He banged down the gavel, then added, "I don't want to see you in my courtroom again."

"The feeling is mutual," Abby muttered under her breath as she and Harry turned to leave. "Thank goodness that's over," she breathed in relief as they left the courthouse. "That judge looked at me like he'd enjoy sending me up the river for a hundred years."

Harry laughed and threw an arm around her shoulders. "Judge Stewart looks at everyone that way. The man has no sense of humor whatsoever."

"I'm glad I'll never have to see him again," Abby exclaimed, thinking once again of his cold, ash-colored eyes.

"Come on, love, I'd better get you home before somebody tries to pick you up again."

"Thanks, I'm anxious to get home," Abby said with a grin. "I can't wait to get my hands on Charley."

Harry laughed. "Just remember, you don't want to wind up back here in front of Judge Stewart again!"

"No," Abby protested, kicking off her high-heeled shoes and sinking down into the worn, overstuffed sofa. She was grateful to have made it through the week. Since the night of her arrest a week ago, her life had been the pits. It seemed as if everything and everyone conspired to make her as miserable as possible. Now her daughter was joining the conspiracy.

"Oh, come on, Mom," Charlene urged, sitting cross-legged on the floor at her mother's feet. "You promised me that one night this week we'd meet Lauren and get pizza for supper."

"Oh, Charley, I know I promised, but not tonight." Abby stretched her arms up over her head and simultaneously wiggled her toes, trying to release the tension from her body. "I've had a horrible day. I swear, there must have been a full moon last night because all the kids were animals today. Jacob Warren confessed that the only reason he read *Romeo and Juliet* was so he could highlight the sexy parts." Abby shook her head with a rueful smile. "I'm afraid Shakespeare disappointed him."

"Jacob Warren is a total nerd," Charley pronounced with all the conviction of a fourteen-year-old. "And if you had a really bad day, then it's a good night to go out to eat. You won't have to mess with cooking, and besides, it's already set up. We're supposed to meet Lauren at the Pizza Palace at seven o'clock."

"Charley, you know how I hate it when you make plans without consulting me," Abby said with a sigh of resignation.

Still, she had promised, and Abby never made her promises lightly. Besides, she'd been hearing about this Lauren for weeks, ever since school started. Charley and Lauren had become inseparable at school and talked on the telephone for hours each evening. Although Abby had seen the two girls together in the halls at school, she had yet to actually meet her daughter's new best friend.

"All right," she relented. "We'll go tonight, but this is the last time I want you presenting me with plans already made."

Charley nodded, her brown eyes shining with excitement. "I promise," she agreed.

"I think I'll go soak in a hot tub and see if I can get relaxed before we go." Abby stood up, ruffling her daughter's dark hair as she walked by.

Once in the tub, she sank into the hot, scented water and sighed. This past week had been the longest of her life. She hadn't told Charley about being picked up and taken to the police station. She had merely told her daughter that Walt was a jerk and the date an unmitigated flop. She also told her daughter that she was never to set Abby up with a date again. She didn't care if the man was Mel Gibson. Abby wasn't interested.

Men... She'd decided she could live without them. Her only marriage had been a complete disaster. The one good thing that had come out of it was Charley.

Besides, her life was rich. She had her job teaching language arts to high school juniors. She had her adult students and she had Charley.

She frowned. It had just been in the past six months that Charley had begun a personal crusade to find Abby a man. When the teenager had suddenly discovered boys, she seemed to realize the lack of a man in her mother's life. What Charley didn't realize was how difficult real love was to come by, and Abby wouldn't settle for less.

She picked up the sponge and ran it lightly over her shoulders and down her full breasts. Still, she had to admit there were times when her body yearned for a man's touch, times when she felt a tension deep within her that she knew only a man could ease. But she'd been burned enough times to be afraid of the fire. Some of the most wonderful men she'd dated had ruined the relationships by merely opening their mouths. They spoke in meaningless platitudes, using overworked phrases and clichés that began with "babe," or "hon."

Her sister had always told her to beware of men who used generic nouns instead of proper names, and Abby wisely took her advice. A grin crossed her features. She was probably the only woman in the world who had been picked up for prostitution and hadn't been with a man for as long as she could remember.

Her smile slowly faded. She'd come to the conclusion that she was much too set in her ways now to become involved with anyone else. She'd been alone for ten years. Her life was well-ordered and peaceful. Why would she want to bring a man into it and muddle everything?

Minutes later she pulled on a pair of jeans as Charley came into her bedroom. "What time did you tell Lauren we'd meet her?" she asked her daughter as she pulled a tan sweater out of the closet.

"Seven." Charley sat down on the edge of the bed. "Why don't you wear that blue sweater I bought for you for your birthday? It makes your eyes look so pretty."

Abby shrugged, hung the tan one back in the closet and took out the light blue sweater. She pulled it on over her head, then went over to the mirror to fix her hair. She brushed her shoulder-length dark waves, then reached for a blue clasp.

"Oh, Mom, why don't you leave it loose?" Charley protested, coming to stand behind Abby. "You look so much prettier when you wear your hair down instead of pulled back in that old-lady bun."

Abby laughed at her daughter's description of her usual hairstyle, but decided to wear her hair loose to please her. "Why are you so concerned with how I look for tonight? Is it so important that I impress Lauren?"

"No..." Charley's gaze didn't quite meet Abby's in the mirror. "I mean, I'm always concerned with how you look."

Abby put down her hairbrush and turned to eye her daughter suspiciously. "Charley, everything is all right, isn't it?"

"Sure, Mom. Why?" Charley met her gaze, but Abby recognized the uneasy glint of evasiveness in her daughter's brown eyes. She should recognize it. She'd seen it often enough in her ex-husband's before their divorce.

"Just wondering." Abby turned and gave her daughter a quick hug, then turned back to the mirror. She knew Charley would eventually tell her whatever it was that was on her mind. If there was one accomplishment Abby was proud of, it was the open, loving relationship she'd managed to foster with her child. Their communication lines worked well, and Abby knew it was just a matter of time before Charley told her what it was that darkened her eyes with secrecy.

Within twenty minutes the two were in the car heading toward the Pizza Palace. "You were right. This is much better than staying home and cooking." Abby smiled at Charley, having resigned herself to the night out and deciding to enjoy the opportunity of spending time with Charley and her new best friend. "So, tell me about Lauren."

"Lauren's terrific. She's funny and smart and just wonderful." Charley smiled widely. "Have you ever met somebody and you know instantly that they're going to be someone special in your life? That's the way it was with Lauren and me. We just clicked."

"It's nice to have a best friend. I know how much you've missed Carrie since she moved away," Abby observed, pulling into a parking space in the crowded lot of the pizza establishment.

"Yeah, I miss Carrie, but I think Lauren and I are going to be even better friends. We're so much alike, and we want the same things." Charley fell silent as they got out of the car. As they reached the door of the restaurant, she spoke again. "Uh... I think Lauren's dad is going to be here with her."

"That's nice. You know I always like to meet the parents of your friends."

Charley smiled uneasily, pausing outside the door. "Mom, promise me you won't get mad."

Abby laughed. "Charley, whenever you say that, I automatically ready myself to get angry. What's going on?" She looked at her daughter curiously.

"Well..." Charley hesitated for a moment. "Lauren's dad is sort of divorced and he's coming tonight just to meet you. He sort of thinks it's a blind date. That's why I wanted you to look especially nice."

And that was the secret she'd seen in Charley's eyes, Abby thought. "Remind me when we get home tonight that you're sort of grounded," Abby said through clenched teeth.

"Somehow I knew you'd react this way," Charley said dismally as they walked into the dim interior of the Pizza Palace. "Look, there's Lauren and her dad," Charley exclaimed.

Abby looked to where her daughter pointed. Instantly the blood drained from her face and her heart lurched with a sickening thud. She saw Lauren, her blond hair shining like a halo in the light from the candle that burned in the middle of the table. But it was the man next to Lauren who made Abby fight an overwhelming impulse to turn and run. Sitting next to Lauren, looking stern and formidable, was the Honorable Judge Eldridge Stewart.

Chapter Two

Judge Eldridge Stewart frowned at his daughter across the table. "I'm quite upset by all this nonsense, Lauren. First you talk me into coming here for supper, then inform me that we're meeting your friend. And now you inform me that this is actually a 'sort of' blind date and I'm really here to meet your friend's divorced mother. Had you told me that in the first place I wouldn't even be here."

"But that's exactly why I didn't tell you in the first place," Lauren explained. Her Kewpie-doll lips turned downward in unhappiness. "Oh, come on, Dad. Please don't be mad at me. I just wanted you to have a little fun."

"I'll choose my own way to have fun, thank you," he returned. And it won't be sitting through a blind date with some husband-hungry divorcée, he thought.

"I just thought it would be cool for you to meet Charley and her mom. After all, Charley has become my very best friend in the whole wide world. Besides—" her frown was replaced with a look of petulance "—you're always complaining because I never introduce you to my friends and their parents."

That was true, he thought reflectively. But he had a feeling Lauren's ultimate goal was not to have him meet her friend, but rather to matchmake between himself and her friend's mother.

Recently his daughter seemed to have made it her mission in life to get him remarried, and he simply wasn't interested. What Lauren didn't understand was that the last thing he wanted in his life was another woman.

He still had a bad taste in his mouth, a bitterness in his heart at the way his marriage to Lauren's mother had fallen apart three years before. He'd learned the hard way that love couldn't be depended on to last, that trust was just an empty promise.

No, he wanted nothing more to do with relationships that involved his heart. It had been battered and bruised enough. The only female he wanted in his life was Lauren, and there were times when he thought she'd drive him crazy before he finally got her raised.

"I don't want you pulling something like this again, young lady," he said sternly to Lauren.

"Okay, okay." She managed to appear contrite, then brightened as she looked across the room. "Hey look, there's Charley and her mom." Lauren squealed with excitement, standing up to wave at the two females who'd just walked through the door.

He watched as they began weaving their way through the tables toward them, the shorthaired, spritelike Charley waving as enthusiastically as Lauren.

He looked at the woman lagging behind the teenager. She was dressed casually in a pair of jeans and a pale blue sweater that showed off her slender shape. Her hair was a curtain of darkness that fell softly to her shoulders. She looked young, far too young to have a daughter Charley's age.

He frowned. He knew her from somewhere. The brilliant blue eyes and delicate features looked vaguely familiar. His mind quickly ran through possibilities... his bank teller... the grocery store clerk... The dark hair is all wrong, he thought illogically. She should have blond hair.

Then it struck him. *Of course, the accidental hooker. That's who she is.* He groaned inwardly. Not only had his daughter tricked him as to why she had wanted him to come, but she'd also managed to fix him up with a woman who, through strange circumstances, had appeared before him in night court the week before. As he recalled, those circumstances had been prompted by a bad blind date. Well, she was about to have another one because he intended to make it abundantly clear that he wasn't interested.

Abby had never fainted before in her life, but at the moment she desperately wished for the oblivion fainting would give her by rescuing her from this dreadful situation. Her ordeal the week before had been an embarrassing incident, one she'd tried desperately to forget.

"Come on, Mom," Charley urged impatiently as Abby lagged behind.

"I'm coming," Abby returned helplessly. The only thing she could hope for was that he wouldn't recognize her. After all, the one and only time he'd seen her she'd been buried beneath a blond wig, tons of makeup and tacky clothing. Maybe he wouldn't recognize her now.

However, as she approached the table and saw the gleam of recognition in his eyes, this hope died and she knew that he knew who she was. A blush swept up to color her cheeks. If only he wouldn't say anything in front of the girls about how they had previously met. She didn't want to have to try to explain that to Charley.

"Hi, Lauren," Charley greeted her friend. "This is my mom, Abby."

"Hi, Mrs. Jones. I've seen you around school about a hundred times. It's nice to finally officially meet you." Lauren offered her a friendly smile.

"And this is my dad, Mac. Well, actually Mac is his nickname. Dad's real name is so gross he only uses it professionally."

Mac stood up and held out his hand to Abby. "Nice to meet you, Mrs. Jones," he said stiffly as he shook her hand.

"Abby, please," she returned with relief, sliding into the seat between Charley and Lauren. Apparently he wasn't going to say anything about their previous meeting.

For a moment there was an awkward silence as the two girls looked at them expectantly. Abby offered the man a tentative smile, one he didn't return. Oh, it's going to be a long night, she thought as she flipped open the menu that lay before her. She was aware of Mac doing the same thing.

"Well, isn't this great?" Lauren exclaimed, looking at her father, then at Abby with a pleased expression.

"Mom, Mr. Stewart is a judge. Isn't that cool?" Charley asked, apparently in an attempt to get the conversational ball rolling.

"It must be a fascinating job," Abby said, deciding at least to try to be civil. After all, it was a matter of circumstances and manipulative teenagers that had thrown them together.

"Not really." He smiled, his coldly perfect features reflecting nothing of the gesture. There followed another awkward silence.

"Don't get Dad started talking about his job." Lauren jumped into the silence. "He loves to talk shop."

Mac merely smiled at his daughter, then returned his interest to the menu. Abby felt her irritation rising. He wasn't even making an attempt to be sociable. It wasn't her fault that she'd been mistakenly nabbed by an overzealous police officer and ended up before him. And it wasn't her fault that her daughter had tricked her into coming to meet him tonight. So why was he treating her as if she had the plague? Why wasn't he even making a stab at civility?

"Dad, Mrs. Jones teaches language arts at the high school," Lauren explained.

He looked at Abby dispassionately. "That must keep you on your toes."

"Not really," she replied coolly, looking back at her menu. Two could play the unsociable game.

At that moment the waitress appeared at their table to take their orders. There was a moment of confusion, but finally it was decided that they would order one king-size pizza and split it. The waitress wrote up the order, then left.

"Mom, can we have a couple of quarters for the jukebox?" Charley motioned to the brightly lit, ultramodern machine across the room.

"Uh... I don't think I have any change," Abby replied, not wanting Charley and Lauren to leave her alone with this self-righteous, silent oaf for even one minute, one second.

"Here, girls, I've got some change." Mac dug into his pocket and extracted several quarters. He handed them to Lauren and she and Charley giggled their way over to the jukebox.

Once again the heavy silence descended around Mac and Abby. She played with her water glass and noticed he found his fingernails utterly fascinating. The silence grew, like a living, breathing thing between them, but Abby steadfastly refused to be the one to break it.

Finally he heaved a heavy sigh and looked at her. "I see you still aren't particularly discriminating when it comes to blind dates." Abby stared at him, so appalled at his audacity she was rendered speechless. "Look," he continued, "I have to be honest with you. I don't know what my daughter or your daughter might have told you about me, but I'm not looking for any kind of a relationship."

"Apparently your dating habits aren't any different from mine," she replied curtly. "After all, you're here, too." She took a deep breath to control her growing aggravation. "I hate to burst your bubble, Judge Stewart, but I'm certainly not looking for a potential husband. In fact, I didn't even know you were going to be here until Charley told me outside in the parking lot. I thought I was coming to meet Lauren and that was all."

He smiled with what Abby assumed was supposed to be apology, but it looked too arrogant to appease her ire. "I was told that this was a date when I sat down at this table. I guess we've both been duped."

"It would seem that we have a couple of mischievous matchmakers in our midst," Abby said, her gaze going over to the two girls who were bent over the jukebox studying the song titles and making their selections.

"It would seem so," he agreed. He looked at her for a moment, his eyes darkly inscrutable. "So what are we going to do about it?"

Abby shrugged. "Make the best of the situation for tonight, then ground them for the rest of their lives when we get them back home."

"Sounds reasonable to me."

Abby studied him for a moment. Stoneface Stewart... she suddenly remembered the nickname Harry had told her. It fitted him. He seemed to be a man who wore his emotions uncomfortably and so preferred not to try them on at all. His face was a stonelike mask, revealing nothing of his thoughts. "I want to thank you for not saying anything in front of the girls about our previous meeting," she said, feeling a warm blush creep up her neck as she remembered her embarrassment of that night in the courtroom. "It's a humiliating experience I want to forget."

He shrugged his broad shoulders. "If I remember correctly, it was simply a matter of your being in the wrong place at the wrong time."

"Yes, sort of like tonight," Abby muttered beneath her breath. She heaved a grateful sigh as the waitress brought their orders. All she wanted to do was eat and leave. Stoneface Stewart was not her idea of a fun date.

Thankfully, as they ate, the two girls chattered about everything from favorite teachers to hairstyles and the latest fashions. What little Mac offered to the conversation only confirmed Abby's opinion that the man was uptight, ultraconservative, and probably very difficult to live with.

It was a shame, really. He was very handsome with his bold features and thick, lightly salted dark hair. His shoulders were wide, his waist too slim to belong to a man who spent most of his time sitting on the bench doing mental exercises. Everything about him looked solid. Yes, she liked the way he looked. Too bad he had the personality of a rock.

She reached for a second piece of pizza at the same time as he did. Their hands touched, both of them pulling away with self-conscious apology. It was really no big deal, an accidental touch between veritable strangers and yet Abby was surprised. She hadn't expected his hand to be so warm, like a cozy fire greeting a cold, weary traveler at the end of a day's journey. It was a shame that the pleasant warmth was wasted on this iceberg of a man, she thought.

"So you teach language arts," he said when the girls had once again gone back to the jukebox and left them alone.

Abby nodded, smiling as she thought of her work. "Yes, I teach the junior class. I also have a class of adults I teach in the evenings."

"Your work with the high school students must be a study in frustration," he observed.

"Sometimes," she admitted. "But then there are times when you know you've connected, made a difference in the way a young person views things. There are times when I introduce a student to a particular piece of literature and his eyes light up and I know that reading is something he might pursue and enjoy the rest of his life." She broke off, flushing with embarrassment. "Perhaps Charley should have warned you about my tendency to become a bore when I discuss my work."

"I find it admirable that you enjoy working with young people. With more adults like you, maybe I wouldn't see so many kids in my courtroom."

"I love my work, both with the kids and the adult class. My work and Charley are all I need." She said it proudly, wanting to make it clear to this man that she had no more use for him than he apparently did for her.

"That's exactly the way I feel. My work keeps me busy and is very satisfying," he agreed.

"I'm happy with my life and it would seem you are with yours." Abby looked over to the two teenagers. "I guess all we have to do is convince our daughters of that fact."

"I intend to be quite persuasive on that subject when I get Lauren home."

"That makes two of us," Abby returned, then looking at her wristwatch, she stood up. "It's getting late. We really should be going." She pulled some money out of her purse, enough to pay for half the bill.

"Oh, don't worry about it. I'll take care of it," he protested.

"No. Despite what our daughters would like to think, this was not a date, and I always pay my own way." She placed the bills on the table. "It was nice seeing you, Judge Stewart." With this, she turned to go.

Mac watched her, noting the sexy sway of her jean-clad bottom. Then, realizing what he was doing, he jerked himself upright and stared into his glass of soda.

She was pretty. Not drop-dead gorgeous or breathtaking, just comfortably pretty. Her dark hair was a thick curtain falling to her shoulders, with wispy bangs kissing her forehead. Her features were ordinary, except for her eyes, bright blue orbs reflecting her inner emotions. It wasn't until she smiled, flashing a single dimple low in her left cheek, that her face was transformed, changing from ordinary to beautiful.

She might be attractive, but she wasn't his type whatsoever. She was too strong, too opinionated, far too independent. She'd probably be a horror to live with, not that he cared.

"So, what did you think of her?" Lauren asked, plopping down in the chair next to him.

"Not my type," he replied.

Lauren made a moue, looking more like her mother than ever. "Oh, Dad, I think you've forgotten what your type is."

"I don't think you should worry about what my type is. Which reminds me, you're grounded for the next week."

"Oh, Dad," Lauren wailed.

"Don't 'oh, Dad' me. You got me here under false pretenses. You lied to me."

"I didn't lie," Lauren protested.

"A lie of omission. It's still punishable by one week of grounding." He ignored her look of misery. "I've told you a dozen times I'm not interested in getting married again. And if I want to date, I'll find my own dates."

"But you never do," Lauren argued.

"That's my business, not yours." He stood up. "Come on, let's go home. I've got some reading to do tonight."

"Why did we have to leave so soon? It's still early," Charley protested the moment they were in the car and headed toward home.

"You know I've got a class early in the morning," Abby answered.

"Yes, but how often do you get to sit down to dinner with a man as great-looking as Lauren's dad? For an old man he's a total hunk."

Abby laughed at her daughter's words. "He's hardly an old man, Charley," she chided. "He can't be much older than me."

Charley looked at her mother slyly. "So, what did you think of him?"

Abby frowned a moment, trying not to hurt her daughter's feelings but wanting to make it clear to her that there was no way she'd get involved with a man as stuffy as Mac Stewart. "He was okay, but we really don't have anything in common."

"How can you know that after only one date?" Charley asked incredulously. "You can't get to know a man over a quick pizza."

"It wasn't a date. Which reminds me, you're grounded for a week."

"Oh, Mom," Charley protested.

"Don't 'oh, Mom' me," Abby returned. "I want you to stop trying to get me remarried. I like my life.

I don't need a man in it. Even if I did, the man I would choose certainly wouldn't be somebody like Mac Stewart." She turned into their driveway, parked the car and turned to her daughter. "I want you to leave my love life alone. Is that understood, Charley?"

Charley nodded.

"Good." Abby patted her daughter's hand, pleased that she and her daughter were in agreement.

The phone was ringing as they stepped through the door. "I'll get it," Charley yelled, running for the phone in her bedroom. She kicked shut her bedroom door and dived across the bed for the receiver. "Hello?"

"Did you get in trouble?" Lauren's voice drifted across the line.

Charley rolled over onto her back and smiled into the telephone. "A week of grounding. How about you?"

"The same, but it was worth it. At least they know each other now."

"Yeah, but I'm not sure it went real great," Charley said hesitantly, winding the phone cord around her thumb as she talked. "Mom insists that she doesn't want a man in her life."

"My dad says the same thing about a woman. But honestly, Charley, when have grown-ups ever known what's best for them?"

Charley giggled. "True," she agreed, releasing her thumb from the cord and rolling over onto her stomach. "But there weren't any instant fireworks between them."

"That's okay," Lauren exclaimed. "I've read all kinds of books about this. True love is supposed to grow slowly. We just have to keep them together long enough for them to realize they belong together."

"I hope you're right," Charley said with a dubious sigh, releasing her thumb from the cord as it began to turn blue.

"I know I'm right," Lauren replied with conviction.

"I just hope this is worth all the grounding I think I'll be getting."

"Believe me, it will be worth it. Just think, if they get married we'll not only be best friends, we'll be sisters!" Lauren exclaimed.

"So, what's the next step?" Charley asked, giggling again as Lauren began to outline their next plan of attack.

Chapter Three

"Come on, Mom. We're going to be late," Charley whispered emphatically, giving Abby the long-suffering facial expression every teenage girl has perfected.

Abby held up one finger to still her daughter and continued talking into the receiver. "Yes, Harry, sometime this week, I promise. Look, I've got to run. Tonight is the first school dance of the year and Charley is anxious that we arrive on time. I'll be in touch." She murmured a goodbye and hung up, then grabbed her purse. "Okay, Charley, I'm ready."

"It's about time," Charley exclaimed, pausing at the mirror on the wall by the front door to check the spiked, moussed ends of her dark hair for the fifteenth time. "What did Harry want?"

"Oh, just to chat. He wants us to have dinner with him one night this week."

"Do we have to?" Charley moaned. "Harry is such a nerd."

"But he's a nice nerd and yes, we do have to," Abby answered firmly. She knew Charley didn't particularly like Harry, who had a tendency to treat the teenager as if she was still eight years old. But Harry had been Abby's lawyer for her divorce, and through the intervening years he was the one nonthreatening male friend in her life. He was a confirmed bachelor and they shared an easy friendship Abby valued.

"Mom." Charley's plaintive sigh pulled Abby from her reverie. "Can we go now?"

Abby nodded and together the two of them left the apartment and got into the car.

"Do I look okay?" Charley asked anxiously, flipping down the visor to peer into the lighted mirror on the back. "Maybe I should have worn the gray sweater instead of this pink one."

"Honey, relax. You look gorgeous. You'll be the belle of the ball."

"I have to look extra good because I'm working at a disadvantage tonight. I'll probably be the only girl there whose mother is one of the chaperons." Charley flipped the visor back up.

"At least this is the only dance this year I have to chaperon," Abby said. "Besides, I'll make a deal with you. The minute we hit the school gym I'll pretend I've never seen you before."

"Just don't make that 'mother look' if you see me dancing with a guy. You know, the one where your eyebrows go up and you grin real wide."

Abby laughed. "I'll do my best to keep the 'mother looks' to a minimum."

As they drove toward the school, Abby felt her daughter's excitement pulsating in the air and she envied the girl her first toe-dipping into the arena of romance. It was such a special time, when the scent of a boy's cologne could produce heart palpitations, when the touch of his hand could make breathing difficult. Oh yes, how well Abby recalled. It was a time of excitement, a time when anything seemed possible.

Abby sighed wistfully as she pulled into the school parking lot. She wished she still believed in the power of romance, the magic of love, but that had all been crushed beneath the weight of a bad marriage. She now knew the effort it took to make relationships work.

"Are you sure I look all right?" Charley's voice broke into Abby's thoughts.

Abby parked the car, then turned and smiled at her daughter. "You look beautiful, honey, and I just know you're going to have a wonderful time tonight." She gave Charley a quick hug.

"Ah, Mom," Charley protested, patting her hair to make sure the hug had done no damage. They got out of the car and as they walked toward the large brick building a group of girls called and waved to Charley.

"Go on with your friends." Abby smiled at her daughter. "I'll meet you at the main gym door when the dance is over."

Charley nodded and ran to join the girls. Abby's smile lingered on her face as she walked into the school gym.

"How can you look so pleasant knowing you're about to be pitted against hundreds of gyrating, hormone-pumping teenagers for the next three hours?" Kerry Landis, the art teacher, came to stand next to Abby.

"What are you doing here? I thought you'd drawn the Christmas dance," Abby asked her curiously.

"I did, but I traded with one of the other teachers. I'm hoping for a Swedish Christmas with a certain blond hunk."

Abby grinned. "That answers my next question. I was going to ask you if you were still seeing Sven."

Kerry laughed. "Honey, I'm doing a lot more than just 'seeing' Sven."

Abby and Kerry had become single at about the same time and for a while following their divorces they had played the singles bar scene together. Abby had grown tired of the game, weary of the lounge lizards who hid wedding rings and were interested merely in a night of uncomplicated sex. Kerry had continued to play, insisting that Mr. Right was going to find her across a crowded, smoke-filled room. It seemed she'd been right. "So, does this mean you've finally found your prince?" Abby asked.

"Maybe," Kerry answered with a small smile. "All I really know is that I had to kiss an awful lot of toads to find Sven. I don't intend to give him up anytime soon." She looked at Abby curiously. "What about you? Any princes in your life?"

"No, I'm still kissing a lot of toads." Abby laughed.

Kerry smiled and looked around. "The gym looks pretty good, doesn't it?" she observed.

"Yes, it does. It's amazing what a little crepe paper, dim lighting and a sparkling crystal ball can do to transform an ordinary gym."

"Too bad they haven't figured out a way to cover up the odor of sneakers," Kerry added with a chuckle. "I'll see you later. I'm supposed to help set out the punch bowl and goodies."

Abby nodded, then leaned against the wall, watching as the gym began to fill up and the band started tuning their instruments on stage. The kids who stopped and spoke to her were all dressed with a little more care than usual. Their eyes sparkled just a little more brightly.

Abby recalled the excitement of the school dances, when magic was in the air and everyone looked different, more attractive than they did in the hallways of the school. She'd always worried that somehow she would end up spending the evening pressed against a wall, hopelessly waiting for some young man to ask her to dance. Her fears had always come to nothing. She'd loved to dance, and most of the boys knew it, and she was rarely without a partner spinning her around on the floor.

She smiled as she saw Charley on the other side of the gym, standing with a group of girls who giggled and shot flirting smiles across the room where some of the boys clustered, trying to seem nonchalant.

As the band began playing at a volume that threatened to curl the ends of her hair, she wandered over to the refreshment table and poured herself a glass of the sweet orange punch. With her eardrums vibrating, she leaned back against the wall, suddenly realizing it was going to be a very long three hours.

Mac Stewart followed reluctantly behind Lauren as they walked across the parking lot toward the school building. He could already hear the music, a loud raucous beat of rock and roll he knew would probably give him a horrendous headache before the end of the night.

He couldn't believe he'd actually agreed to Lauren's pleas that he chaperon the dance this evening. He wanted to be a part of Lauren's life, but surely there was a better way than this.

As they entered the gymnasium and he got the full benefit of the five-piece band on stage, he felt the beginnings of the anticipated headache tingling over his left eyebrow.

"There's my friends," Lauren squealed, causing the throb over his eye to intensify. "I'll see you later, Dad. Have fun." She waved to him over her shoulder, then ran to join her group of friends.

Mac leaned back against the wall, feeling ancient as he watched the limber, youthful bodies dancing energetically to the throbbing rhythm.

Still he wasn't sorry he'd come. He was determined to be a part of Lauren's life, maintain a firm hand so she wouldn't spin out of control as so many teenagers did. God knew, he saw enough of those kids in his courtroom.

His eyes scanned the room, finding his daughter in a group of girls that included her best friend, Charley.

Instantly he thought of Abby and the "blind date" they'd shared the week before. He hadn't thought about her all week, but now he found himself wondering if she was here tonight.

Then he saw her, standing alone near the refreshment table. She was looking off to the side, not in his direction, and he took the opportunity to study her more closely. The glittering crystal ball suspended from the ceiling of the gym caused tiny stars of light to dance in her dark hair, which was pulled demurely back at the nape of her neck. Her profile was sharp and well-defined, offering him a view of the straight line of her nose, the slight protrusion of cheekbone, the graceful column of her neck.

Again he was struck by the fact that Abby Jones was a very attractive woman. It was an assessment made on an intellectual level, one he refused to allow to impact him on an emotional plane.

He hesitated, unsure if he should walk over and talk to her or not. On the one hand, it was going to be a long couple of hours if he was going to spend the time leaning against the wall like an overgrown wallflower. On the other hand, he worried that if he went over to her and struck up a conversation she might misconstrue his intentions, assume he was expressing an interest in her. That was certainly the last thing he wanted.

In any case, the decision was taken out of his hands, for at that moment she turned and saw him. A small smile played on her lips as she approached him.

"Well, well. What brings you here tonight, Judge Stewart?" she asked.

"Mac, please," he returned. "And Lauren brings me here. She talked me into chaperoning tonight, but I'm really not sure exactly what my duty is as a chaperon," he admitted.

"You're doing just fine," she assured him. "Your only real task as a chaperon is to stand around and look...uh...adult." She'd been about to say stern, which was exactly how he looked, but she'd amended it to a less harsh description.

"What about you? How did you get roped into being here?" he asked.

"Actually, I'm on duty. Each teacher is required to chaperon one school dance each year. This one is mine."

"I suppose there are drawbacks to every job."

"I really don't mind this," she protested. "There's something very reassuring about school dances. It's one of the few things that don't change with the years." She smiled up at him. "Can't you feel it in the air? An electricity, an excitement? These kids are growing up right here, right now, before our eyes. The girls are practicing their newfound flirtation skills and the boys are learning the appropriate responses. They're all going to be just a little more comfortable in their own sexuality after tonight."

"I'm not sure I want Lauren comfortable with her own sexuality," he replied dryly.

"You don't mean that," Abby returned with a laugh. "How about a cup of punch?"

He shrugged. "Sure."

As she dipped them each a cup of punch, she found herself studying him, admiring his physical appeal. There was such a clear-cut masculinity about him. The spattering of silver at his temples, rather than aging him or giving him a touch of vulnerability, only added to his overall appearance of strength and dignity. Of course, part of this aura of dignity came from the fact that she'd first seen him in his somber black robes, and each time after that in a dark suit and white shirt. She found it difficult to imagine him in casual attire.

"God, this stuff is horrible," he exclaimed after taking a sip of the punch.

"Hey, that's my mother's very own recipe you're maligning." Kerry joined them, looking at Mac with mock outrage, then grinned. "Unfortunately, I had to leave out most of the ingredients that give the punch its punch, if you know what I mean." She smiled in open friendliness. "Abby, aren't you going to introduce me to your friend?"

"Of course. Kerry Landis, this is Judge Eldridge Stewart, Lauren Stewart's father."

"Nice to meet you, Judge Stewart."

"Mac," he corrected her, shaking the hand she held out.

"Lauren's a great kid," Kerry said. "I've got her in my second-hour art class. She shows some real natural talent in graphic design."

"I wish she'd show a little more talent for math and history," he returned.

Kerry smiled. "That's a sentiment I often hear expressed from parents. Still, Lauren is a good kid. Now, if you'll excuse me, I think it's time for a bathroom check."

"Bathroom check?" he repeated blankly.

"We're supposed to check the rest rooms every half hour or so and make sure nobody is fighting or smoking," Kerry explained. "Nice meeting you, Mac. See you guys later." With a little wave, she moved away from them and across the room.

Abby and Mac threw away their paper cups and Abby offered him another friendly, but slightly uncomfortable smile. She felt like one of the kids, working at socializing with a member of the opposite sex for the very first time. She wasn't even sure she liked Mac Stewart very much, wasn't sure he was worth the effort of making conversation.

"How do they stand this music?" he asked, breaking into the uncomfortable silence. "All I'm getting from it is a terrific headache."

"You don't like it?" Somehow this didn't surprise Abby. "I suppose you like classical."

"What's wrong with that?" he asked defensively.

Abby merely shrugged. She'd just about decided to excuse herself and leave him when Lauren and Charley joined them.

"Hi, guys, having a good time?" Lauren asked, looking first at her father, then at Abby, a sparkle of excitement in her eyes.

Both Abby and Mac shrugged noncommittally.

"How come you haven't danced yet? The band is awesome," Charley declared.

"Yeah, Dad, why don't you ask Mrs. Jones to dance?" Lauren looked at her dad expectantly. "They're even playing a slow song for you old folks."

Abby felt her cheeks flush slightly as she saw Mac's discomfort.

"Come on, you two... dance!" The girls pushed the two adults toward the dance floor.

"I'd better warn you, I'm not very good at this sort of thing," Mac said as he took Abby into his arms.

He was right. He wasn't very good at it. He moved his feet very little, his body even less. He swayed more than danced, as if his feet had no spontaneity, no creativity.

Yet Abby found herself enjoying the simple act of being in his arms. He smelled nice, like coffee beans and autumn nights with a subtle hint of a spiced after-shave.

Again she was struck by the leanness of his physique. Beneath the dark jacket she could feel his taut shoulder muscles under her hands. He had the sort of solid build that was comfortable for cuddling, a body made to be accommodating.

She was more aware of him than she could ever remember being of a man. Perhaps it was the setting, a high school dance, throwing her back to a time when her senses were sharper, her perceptions more highly tuned to members of the opposite sex. It was as if she was rediscovering her own sexuality at the age of thirty-four.

She tilted back her head so she could see his face. The whirling mirrored ball overhead caused pinpoints of starry lights to highlight the silver that dusted his temples. The dim lighting emphasized the strong lines of his jaw, the shadow of a heavy beard shaved close.

She shut her eyes, easily able to imagine the feel of his whiskers against the softness of her skin, rubbing erotically against her neck, her cheeks, her lips. Her eyes flew open with shock as she realized the direction her thoughts were taking her.

Mac felt a light sheen of perspiration break out across his forehead. It had been three years since he'd held a woman in his arms and he'd forgotten what a pleasurable sensation it could be. The scent of her reminded him of peaches freshly picked, eaten while standing in an orchard, the juices running down his arm. Her breasts snuggled comfortably against his chest, making him aware of her heartbeat echoing his own.

He had a sudden insane desire to kiss the skin right behind her ear which seemed to be one of the sources of the entrancing peach scent. His sudden desire surprised him. He'd thought that particular emotion was dead. But he really shouldn't be surprised, he thought. He was a healthy, normal man with physical needs...needs he'd tried to ignore for the past three years.

He breathed a sigh of relief as the song came to an end. He released her immediately, not wanting her soft curves or sweet scent anywhere near him for any longer. He'd gone a long time without feeling the stirring of desire, and he certainly wasn't going to act on them now, especially with a woman he wasn't even sure he liked.

"Thanks," she murmured, her gaze not quite meeting his. "I...uh...I think I'll do a rest room check." With a slight nod, she turned and left him standing at the edge of the dance floor.

Once in the rest room Abby got a wet paper towel and ran it lightly across her flushed face. She felt both hot and cold at the same time. "Hang a spinning ball from the ceiling and you turn into a sappy fool," she told her reflection in the mirror.

Sure, it had felt good to be held in his arms, but it probably would have felt just as good being in any male's arms, she rationalized. It had been a very long time since she'd had the pleasure of feeling strong arms enfold her close, hearing a heartbeat talking intimately to her own.

Mac Stewart was a stuffy old coot who never cracked a smile. He looked at everyone as if they were potential criminals. Surely even Judge Roy Bean, the notorious judge of the Old West, had managed a laugh every now and then.

That single moment, when she'd suddenly found herself imagining what Mac's lips would feel like on hers, when she'd wondered how his whiskers would feel rubbing against her skin... it had simply been a matter of underused hormones letting her know they were still there, still kicking. But if she were going to feed her starving hormones, it certainly wouldn't be with somebody as uptight and stuffy as Mac Stewart.

With this thought firmly in mind, she patted her face once again, checked to make certain her cheeks were no longer flushed, then went out to rejoin the dance. After she entered the gym, her gaze automatically searched the room for Mac.

She finally spotted him standing against the wall, once again looking grim and forbidding. Everything fell back into perspective for Abby. That single moment on the dance floor when she'd imagined the feel of his lips against hers had been nothing but a strange anomaly. The odds of it happening again were astronomical.

"Okay, spill your guts."

Abby whirled around to see Kerry eyeing her suspiciously. "Spill my guts about what?"

"About where you met Mr. Hunk over there." She moved her eyebrows in Mac's direction.

Abby smiled, thinking of what Kerry's expression would be if Abby told her about the very first time she'd met Mac. That story certainly would keep the school gossipmongers happy for months. "Charley and Lauren sort of set up a blind date for us last week."

"Lucky you. I never had a blind date as sexy-looking as Judge Stewart." She grinned slyly. "He definitely looks like prince material to me."

Abby laughed. "Don't let him fool you. He may look like prince material, but underneath that sexy exterior the man is pure toad."

"Hmm, too bad. The man scores high on the 'easy on the eyes' meter." Kerry frowned across the room. "I could swear I just saw smoke coming from Joshua Billiard's mouth, and I have a feeling it's not from dancing too much." With a wave, Kerry took off across the dance floor to accost the errant Joshua who was trying to hand a smoldering cigarette to anyone who would take it.

With a sigh, Abby checked her watch. Another hour to go. She leaned back against the wall and watched the kids, hoping the hour went fast.

"What happened?" Charley asked Lauren. The two girls stood in a corner of the gym, eyeing Abby and Mac. "I thought we had them. They were dancing and smiling and everything looked great, but now they're standing against different walls and aren't even looking at each other."

Lauren frowned. "They're harder cases than I thought." She shoved a strand of her shining blond hair behind her shoulder, a frown causing her nose to wrinkle. "This is going to take some creative manipulation."

"Like what?" Charley asked, grinning at her friend curiously.

Lauren's frown deepened. "I'm not sure. We need some time to come up with a foolproof plan.

There has to be a way to get them together with nobody else around and plenty of time for them to fall in love."

"Sounds like a tall order to me," Charley said, her smile fading into glumness. "Maybe we should just forget the whole thing."

"Don't you want to be my sister?" Lauren asked.

"Well sure... but..."

"Don't be a quitter." With a wide grin, Lauren threw her arm around Charley. "Have faith in me and my schemes, Charley. Why don't we see if I can spend the night with you after the dance. That way we'll have all night long to come up with a way to make my dad and your mom fall in love."

"Okay, and even if we don't come up with a master plan, we can talk about how gross Susan Willey looks in that dress and I'll tell you how Brandon Walker kisses."

"You kissed Brandon Walker?" Lauren squealed with excitement. "Where? When?"

Charley laughed. "Come on, let's go ask my mom if you can stay the night, then I promise I'll tell you about Brandon."

Chapter Four

Abby opened her eyes, squinting against the early morning sun that danced through her lacy bedroom curtains, making pretty patterns of light on her bedspread. Shoving her hair away from her face, she rolled over and looked at her clock radio. Eight o'clock. She groaned and turned back over, closing her eyes once again.

A loud knock on the front door caused her to sit straight up. As she jumped out of bed and stumbled to the door, she realized it must have been a previous knock that had initially awakened her. Who on earth would be at her door at this ungodly hour on a Saturday morning?

She peered through the peephole, gasping in surprise as she saw Mac standing on the other side of the door. "Uh... just a minute," she yelled, scurrying back into the bedroom for her robe. Mac had said last night at the dance that he'd be by early to get Lauren, but eight o'clock on a Saturday morning was practically obscene.

She hurried back to the door, belting her robe and finger combing her tousled hair. "Mac," she greeted him, opening the door to let him in.

"Oh, I woke you," he observed, looking stiff and self-conscious as he moved to stand just inside the door.

"Yes, well, when you said last night that you'd be here early to get Lauren, I guess I thought you meant early afternoon." She motioned for him to follow her into the kitchen. "Why don't you have a seat and I'll fix you a quick cup of coffee. It will take a few minutes for the girls to get up and around."

"Please don't go to any trouble," he protested, sitting down at the round oak table.

"No trouble," she assured him, efficiently placing coffee and water into the coffee machine. Almost immediately the smell of the fresh brew filled the air. "I'll just go wake up the girls," Abby said, flashing him a quick smile, then hurrying from the room.

Mac breathed a shaky sigh when she'd gone. He hadn't been prepared for the sudden surge of desire he'd felt for her when she'd opened the door to greet him. With her dark hair in charming disarray and the fuzzy blue robe that caressed her curves and exactly matched the shade of her eyes, she'd awakened those crazy emotions once again.

Twice in as many days she'd managed to stir the embers of a fire he'd thought gone out—first at the dance last night as he'd held her close in his arms, and now in a damned blue robe that concealed more than it revealed.

What was wrong with him? There were many women who passed in and out of his life on a daily basis—attorneys, law clerks, any number of attractive females, but none of them affected him quite like Abby Jones. What was wrong with him? He repeated the question. Why did he react this way to a woman who was nothing to him except his daughter's best friend's mother?

It surprised him, feeling this way again. It had been so long since he'd felt much of anything except anger and bitterness. This was something new, and just a little bit frightening.

He focused his attention on the room where he sat, uncomfortable with his inner thoughts. It was a pleasant kitchen with personal touches that radiated warmth and cheerfulness. A copper kettle sat on the stovetop, slightly tarnished with use but catching the radiance of the sunshine that poured through the yellow curtains at the window. She must drink a lot of tea, he thought. He hated hot tea.

Still, the hominess of the kitchen made him think about his own. When Melinda had left him three years before, he'd sold their big house and had bought a smaller one where no memories lingered to haunt him. But suddenly he realized that he'd done little to make the place a reflection of himself or Lauren. Each room was functional, but without flavor. The only room in the entire house that had any character was Lauren's room, decorated with pictures and posters, memorabilia and stuffed animals that reflected the teenager's personality.

"Sorry it took so long," Abby said, coming back into the kitchen and pulling him from his reverie. "I was afraid I might have to set off a bomb to get them up," she explained as she poured two mugs full of coffee and joined him at the table. "Although it's all my fault. I kept the girls up indecently late last night."

"You kept them up?" He looked at her in surprise.

"Guilty as charged," she returned. "After we got home last night from the dance I got a craving for homemade pizza. So at midnight I had the girls cutting up mushrooms and green peppers. I didn't think about Lauren needing to wake up so early."

"I generally don't like Lauren to sleep too late on the weekends," Mac said, pausing a moment to take a sip of his coffee. "I don't like her getting off schedule."

"I've always thought being off schedule was a normal rite of passage for a teenager," Abby said dryly. "Even I'm guilty of being a lazy slug on Saturday mornings. There's nothing I like better than spending half the day in bed with a cup of coffee and the morning newspaper."

Mac could easily envision her beneath crisp sheets, clad in a lacy white nightgown, the top of which peeked out above her loosely belted robe. It was a disturbing image, one that immediately put him on the defensive. "I've always been a firm believer in the adage that the early bird gets the worm."

"On Saturdays even worms sleep in," she returned smoothly, her quick wit bringing an unaccustomed smile to his face.

"Touché," he said, allowing the smile to linger for only a moment before he took another drink of coffee.

"Are you on your way to work this morning?" she asked, gesturing to his suit and tie.

"Not officially, but I often spend Saturdays at the courthouse catching up on paperwork and listening to some of the other judges at work."

Abby made a face. "Not me. On Saturdays I don't even think about work. I try to do things that are as far removed as possible from school and students."

Mac shrugged. "I guess it's a matter of levels of commitment."

"I'm very committed to my work, but I think it's rather a matter of balance." A spark of challenge glittered in her gaze. "You know what they say about all work and no play...."

Before he had a chance to respond, Lauren and Charley stumbled into the kitchen, both of them looking groggy and more than half-asleep.

"Here they are, our little rays of sunshine," Abby said, getting up from the table and reaching out to tousle Charley's hair.

"Ah, Mom," Charley grumbled, stepping away from Abby's caress.

"How come you had to come so early?" Lauren asked her dad, flopping into the chair next to him and shoving her tangled blond hair out of her eyes.

"I've got work to do this morning," Mac told her, then drained the last of the coffee from his cup.

"You're always working, that's all you ever do," Lauren complained. "You'd better watch out, Dad, or you're going to turn into a workaholic bore."

The words, so close to what Abby had intimated just before the girls had entered the kitchen, caused a small smile to curve her lips. As she saw Mac's thunderous expression, she quickly swallowed the grin. "Would you like another cup of coffee?" she asked, not surprised when he shook his head and stood up.

"No, thank you, we really need to be going." Abby walked with them to the front door. "I appreciate your having Lauren over for the night," he said, prodding Lauren with an elbow.

"Oh yeah, thanks, Mrs. Jones. I had a great time," Lauren quipped on cue. "Call me," she said to Charley as she and Mac headed out the door.

Charley nodded her assent, then stumbled back into her bedroom where Abby knew she would probably be in bed until noon.

Once Mac and Lauren had gone, Abby went back into the kitchen and poured herself another cup of coffee. She then sat down at the table, her thoughts on the two who had just left.

Imagine not allowing a teenager to sleep in on a Saturday morning because it might throw her off schedule. Wasn't that some form of child abuse? Abby grinned at her own thoughts. Okay, so it wasn't child abuse, but it did seem excessive.

In the times she'd seen father and daughter together, she'd seen very little real warmth and affection displayed between them. Oh, it was obvious Lauren adored her dad. She had talked about him in glowing terms while they'd made pizza the night before. But Abby had a feeling Mac was a difficult man to please, that Lauren often felt her father's censure and that he held the reins very tightly. Still, she couldn't deny the fact that he was extremely handsome and he always smelled so nice. Even now his scent lingered here in the kitchen, a pleasant, masculine odor.

She stared into her mug reflectively. His smile had surprised her. Although it had been fleeting, a quicksilver expression, it had lightened his eyes and softened the lines of his face. It was a shame he didn't do it more often. It was a smile that promised warmth.

"An empty promise," she murmured, getting up from the table and rinsing the two coffee mugs in the sink. Mac Stewart had about as much warmth as a snowflake in a freezer. She placed the cups in the dish drainer and shoved thoughts of Mac and his daughter out of her mind.

If she was lucky she could squeeze in another couple of hours of sleep before Charley got up and remembered Abby had promised to take her shopping for a new pair of jeans.

"Did you have a good time?" Mac asked as he drove Lauren home.

"Super," Lauren answered, stifling a yawn with the back of her hand. "Mrs. Jones is so cool. We made pizza when we got home from the dance last night. It tasted terrific."

"So she told me," Mac answered.

Lauren grinned. "But I'll bet she didn't tell you that we played rock and roll records and she taught us how to do a bunch of old dances like the stroll and the swim. Then she French-braided my hair, but I had to take it out to sleep." Lauren sighed happily. "It was like having a slumber party with two friends instead of one."

Mac frowned. "It sounds to me like you were up much too late. You'll probably need to get to bed earlier tonight to make up for the loss of sleep."

Lauren groaned. "Oh, Dad, honestly. You still treat me like I'm six years old."

There were times when Mac wished she was still six years old. At six Lauren had been so uncomplicated. It had been easy to relate to her. At that age all it took to make her smile was a tickle to her ribs or a tweak of her nose. But now Mac wasn't sure how to deal with his teenage daughter. She was often moody, unpredictable, an alien who had suddenly taken up occupancy in his daughter's body.

He felt almost jealous as he thought of Lauren's night with Abby. There was something evocative about the vision his mind produced. The scent of fresh, baking pizza, old rock and roll tunes filling the air, the three of them laughing and dancing together—it was a vision that for some reason filled him with an aching loneliness.

"Dad?" Lauren's voice pulled him from his thoughts. She looked at him hesitantly.

"What?" he asked, pulling the car into their driveway.

"How would you like to go camping next weekend with Mrs. Jones and Charley?"

"I wouldn't," he answered easily. He hated camping.

"Oh, come on, Dad. It would be fun." Lauren sat up in the seat and looked at him appealingly.

"Lauren, the last thing in the world I would actually choose to do would be to go camping."

Lauren flopped back and puffed a sigh. "I knew you would say that. Mrs. Jones said there was no way you'd agree to go."

"She did?" Mac felt a faint jab of irritation. "Exactly what did Mrs. Jones say?"

Lauren shrugged. "She just said that you weren't exactly the type to go out and have any fun, that you'd probably prefer to stay home with your nose stuck in some dusty old law book."

"A dusty old law book...!" Mac tightened his grip on the steering wheel despite the fact that the car was parked, the engine shut off.

First there had been the dig about all work and no play, and now this. Mac felt a tic of irritation throbbing in his jaw. What was the woman trying to do? Make him look like a jerk in front of his daughter? And a dull jerk at that!

Decision made, he faced his daughter with a tight smile. "You tell Abby and Charley Jones that if they're game for a weekend camping trip, then we're game as well."

Lauren stared at him in disbelief for a long moment, then with a whoop of joy she threw her arms around his neck.

"I just don't like them," Charley said, turning around in front of the dressing-room mirror, looking critically at the jeans she had on.

Abby sagged against the wall, exhausted by the past two hours of shopping. She'd had no idea that jeans came in so many styles and colors. What had begun as the simple task of buying new jeans had taken on the dimensions of searching for Noah's ark. "What's wrong with them?" she asked wearily.

"They're too baggy in the legs," Charley said, frowning once again at her reflection.

"Charley, we've been to three different stores. You must have tried on twenty pairs of jeans."

"Let's just try one more place," Charley urged, unbuttoning the jeans and stepping out of them, then pulling on the pair she'd originally worn. "I saw a great pair, exactly what I want, at Boswell's Boutique. They always carry awesome clothes."

"Then why didn't we try there first?" Abby asked in exasperation.

Charley shot her a quick grin. "I had to make sure I wouldn't like anything better in any other store. Isn't that what they mean by comparison shopping?"

Abby groaned. "Come on, let's go to Boswell's, and if you don't find what you want there then you'll be going without."

Ten minutes later Charley stood in front of the mirrors in the dressing room at Boswell's, a pleased expression on her face as she eyed her reflection. "I knew they'd be perfect," she said, referring to the gray-black jeans that hugged her slender shape to perfection.

"Thank you," Abby said, looking heavenward. "Take them off and I'll go pay for them."

"Mom, what would you think about going camping next weekend?" Charley asked as she changed clothes.

Despite her weariness, Abby laughed. "Why on earth would I want to go camping? I hate camping." She looked at her daughter curiously. "What brought this all on?"

Charley shrugged. "Aunt Becky takes her kids camping all the time."

Again Abby laughed. "I've often told you I think my sister is an aberration. Anyone who actually enjoys sleeping in a tent on the hard ground has got to be a little crazy."

"But Lauren and I thought it would be so much fun," Charley replied.

"Whoa, what does Lauren have to do with this?"

"She and I thought it would be a lot of fun for the four of us to go up to Lake Jackson for the weekend. We could do a little fishing and hiking."

"Camping isn't exactly my idea of a fun way to spend a weekend," Abby said. And camping with Mac Stewart was right up there with a visit to the dentist or cleaning the bathroom, she thought.

Charley sighed. "I guess Judge Stewart was right after all," she muttered.

"Right about what?" Abby's interest immediately perked up.

"Oh nothing, it's not important," Charley replied, then added, "It was just something Lauren told me he said."

"Well, what was it?" Abby asked impatiently.

Charley looked sheepishly at her mom. "He just said that there was no way you'd want to go camping. He said you just weren't the wholesome type who'd enjoy being out in the fresh air with nature."

"Oh he did, did he?" Abby fumed inwardly for a moment. The very nerve of that man, making snap judgments about what she would or wouldn't enjoy. Not wholesome enough? She'd give him wholesome. She'd be so darned wholesome she'd make him sick!

"Charley, you tell Lauren and her father that we'd be happy to go camping with them next weekend."

Charley jumped up and down with excitement, squealing at a decibel that could shatter glass.

"Come on, let's pay for these jeans," Abby said. "I need to get home and call Becky to see if we can borrow all their camping equipment."

Again Charley squealed with excitement and threw her arms around Abby. "You wait and see, Mom. This is going to be a totally awesome weekend."

Oh yeah, it was going to be awesome, all right, Abby thought. She was afraid it was going to be an awesome mess.

"I can't believe you're actually going camping. We've been trying to get you to come with us for years," Becky said to Abby the next evening. Abby had stopped by after work to pick up all the camping equipment she would need for the weekend.

"I still can't quite believe it myself," Abby confessed as Becky added two sleeping bags to the growing pile in the center of the garage floor.

"So where are you guys headed?"

"We thought we'd drive up to Lake Jackson," Abby replied. She was perched on the back of the riding lawn mower, watching Becky dig through the overcrowded garage shelves. "Do we really need all that stuff?" she asked as Becky retrieved a box of cooking utensils.

Becky nodded. "Lake Jackson is a great choice. It's one of our favorite places. It has nice, clean facilities and the fishing is terrific."

"All I know is, that's where Charley and Lauren wanted to go, so that's where we're going."

"Lauren? Who's she?"

"Charley's new best friend. They met at the beginning of school this year and really hit it off. We're going this weekend with her and her father."

Becky's dark eyebrows shot up in curiosity. "Her father? That sounds cozy." She paused a moment, then asked nonchalantly, "Is he single?"

Abby nodded. "Divorced."

The eyebrows climbed higher, threatening to leave Becky's head. "Attractive?"

Abby hesitated. "Yes, I suppose some women would consider Judge Stewart attractive."

"Judge Stewart, as in 'here comes da judge'?" Abby nodded. "Whew." Becky whistled beneath her breath. "Single, attractive and with a great job. Why aren't you marrying him instead of just going camping with him?"

Abby laughed. "I'm not even sure I like the man," she returned. "I'm only going this weekend because I feel personally challenged to prove the man wrong about some things."

"Sounds fascinating," Becky observed, resuming her search of the garage shelves for more equipment.

"I don't know how fascinating it is," Abby returned, eyeing the mountain of gear on the floor. "In fact, I've just been sitting here wondering exactly how and when it happened."

"How and when what happened?" Becky asked curiously.

"Exactly how and when I lost my mind and agreed to this madness," Abby replied dryly.

Chapter Five

Abby's footsteps rang hollowly as she made her way across the marble floor of the courthouse. The main lobby was deserted except for a janitor who desultorily pushed a broom back and forth across the shining floor. He didn't even look at her as she hurried past, heading for the elevators where she punched the up button and checked her watch. Ten minutes after five. The city offices all closed at five and it was obvious the employees didn't hang around for overtime. There was an empty feel to the building that was slightly unsettling.

She breathed a sigh of relief as she arrived on the third floor where the courtrooms were situated. Although one of the rooms was empty, from behind the closed doors of the second one she could hear the murmur of voices.

Cautiously she opened the doors and slid in, taking a seat in the back of the courtroom. She looked around, surprised at the number of people apparently waiting their turn before the judge. Mac sat on the bench, his attention focused on the lawyer before him, who was obviously pleading someone's case.

Abby once again looked at her watch. She was a few minutes early. When Mac had called the night before to set up this meeting, he'd said that court usually recessed for supper about five-thirty. According to her watch, they should be breaking in about the next fifteen minutes.

She settled back on the hard bench and watched the proceedings going on before her. From what she could discern, the lawyer before Mac was defending a woman arrested for shoplifting. As he spoke, Abby studied Mac. He looked so stately in the black robe, his face schooled in dignity. He looked distant, unreachable, as if his heart was molded from tempered steel, unbreakable, unmeltable and immune to emotion of any kind.

She'd been a fool to be goaded into the weekend camping trip. She'd responded to a challenge in an adolescent fashion, following impulse instead of intellect. She should have said no to the trip and spent the weekend in bed with a good romance novel. However, it was too late to back out now.

She sighed and refocused her attention on the lawyer who seemed to finally be winding down.

"Yes, Your Honor, my client is guilty of shoplifting," the lawyer said. "However, circumstances drove her to this criminal activity. Her husband left her and their four children a year ago. Six months ago she lost her home, and since that time she and the children have been living in a car, trying to survive a day-to-day existence." The lawyer paused a moment for effect, then continued. "Judge Stewart, this woman is not a criminal. She's a desperate mother asking for help."

Mac leaned back in his chair, his features looking like they'd been carved in stone. *He's going to throw her in jail,* Abby guessed. *He won't care about her children or her dire circumstances. As far as he's concerned, guilty is guilty.*

Abby sat forward, caught up in the real-life drama unfolding before her. The defendant in the case sat at the defense table, looking young and vulnerable. As Mac asked the defendant to rise and face him, Abby felt her breath catch in her throat.

"Mary Roberts, you have been charged with shoplifting and have pleaded guilty. Your lawyer has explained the extenuating circumstances. Because of these circumstances, I will suspend your sentence on the charge, but with several conditions." He paused a moment, his gaze not straying from the defendant, who shivered beneath the intensity of his eyes. Abby, too, shivered with empathy, remembering the compelling authority his eyes had held when she'd been a defendant before him.

"My conditions are that you contact health and social services and check yourself and your children into a shelter. I want you out of that car and off the streets." He turned and looked at the woman's lawyer. "Mr. Blakemore, you will take care of the details. I want a written report a month from now stating where the family is living and how they are managing." Mac looked back at the defendant. "And I don't want to see you in my courtroom again." He brought the gavel down with a bang. Then, looking at his wristwatch, he announced the dinner break and disappeared through a doorway behind him.

Abby sat for a moment, wondering what she was supposed to do. Had Mac seen her come in? Did he know she was here? Should she go and knock on the door through which he'd disappeared?

At that moment the court bailiff approached her. "Judge Stewart instructed me to bring you to him," he explained.

Abby nodded and followed the bailiff through the doorway and into a small office where Mac sat at a large walnut desk. He rose as she came into the room, offering her a distracted smile. She noticed he'd changed from his black robe into a tailored suit. "Let me just put these files away and we can go." He picked up several manila folders and filed them into the metal cabinet behind the desk.

"There's a coffee shop next door. I hope you don't mind if we grab something there while we finalize the weekend plans. This hour recess is the only one I'll get this evening and I haven't eaten since noon."

"That sounds fine," Abby agreed. "I'm on a tight schedule myself. I have an adult education class at seven."

He ushered her out a back door that brought them out by the elevators. As they walked, she caught the scent of him, the pleasant smell that made her think of warming brandy and wintry nights.

"So it seems we have a camping trip planned," Mac said as they rode the elevator down to the lobby.

"Yes, it sounds great to me." Having committed herself to following through on the plan, Abby mustered up a dose of false enthusiasm. She'd be damned if she'd let him know she hated camping.

"Lauren mentioned something about Lake Jackson. Is that all right with you?" he asked as they left the courthouse and walked out into the cool evening air.

"Sure, Lake Jackson is great. The public facilities are nice and the fishing is terrific," Abby said, merely repeating what Becky had told her the night before.

The conversation was cut short when they entered the busy coffee shop.

As they made their way toward a booth in the back, Abby was surprised by how many people greeted Mac. The greetings were friendly but respectful, and Abby guessed that most of the people who frequented the coffee shop were employees from the courthouse or in the legal arena.

"I hope you don't mind sitting here in the back," Mac said as they sat down in the booth. "I generally try to keep a low profile in here, otherwise my dinner time is interrupted by various acquaintances."

"This is fine," Abby assured him.

Before they could resume the conversation they had begun moments before, the waitress appeared at their table. "Evening, Judge. The usual?" she asked, her brown eyes flirting impudently.

"That's fine, Cindy," Mac returned, handing the young woman his menu. "Abby, what would you like?"

Abby quickly scanned the menu, then settled on a chicken salad sandwich and a glass of iced tea.

Cindy took her menu and smiled again at Mac. "I'll be right back with your coffee, Judge Stewart," she said, the flirtatious sparkle back in her eyes.

Of course, Abby couldn't blame the young woman for being stimulated by Mac. She couldn't deny the fact that he looked exceptionally attractive this evening in a charcoal gray suit that exactly matched his eyes. He looked like he could have been the cover model for a magazine—the up-and-coming, attractive judge. The waitress probably hadn't been around him enough to realize he had the personality of a fence post, Abby thought wryly.

"Then we're agreed on Lake Jackson?" he asked, bringing the conversation back to the original topic and purpose of their meeting.

"That's fine with me," Abby agreed easily. "The girls want to leave late on Friday afternoon. Will that work with your schedule?"

He nodded. "I work morning court on Friday. I get off about three. What about you?"

"I get home from school about three-thirty. I can be ready to go anytime after that," she explained.

"Why don't I pick you and Charley up about five? There's no reason for us to take two vehicles."

Abby agreed reluctantly, although she didn't look forward to being cooped up with him in the small confines of a car for an hour-and-a-half drive. Still, it would be ridiculous for them to drive separately. "What do you want to do about the food?"

Mac frowned a moment. "Why don't you bring the breakfast food and I'll bring the suppers, then we can both bring sandwich meats for lunches," he suggested.

"Sounds reasonable."

The waitress appeared with their orders, placing before Mac a hot roast beef dinner, and Abby's sandwich in front of her. "Can I get you anything else?" she asked, pouring Mac's coffee, then handing Abby her glass of tea.

"No thanks. I think we're fine." Mac smiled at the waitress and again Abby was struck by the power and warmth of the gesture. Too bad he offered it so rarely.

As they ate, a heavy silence settled around them, making Abby sorry she'd decided to stay and eat with him. They'd already finalized the weekend plans and there seemed nothing more to say.

We're two adults, Abby chided herself. *Surely we can carry on a pleasant conversation like civilized people.* But she sensed a barrier, a man-made, Mac-erected barrier that discouraged idle pleasantries of any kind.

Although Abby considered herself to be an extrovert, there was something about Mac's demeanor that dampened any desire to reach out and try to breach that barrier.

She finished her sandwich, sipping her tea as he finished eating. She found her attention wandering as she sat beneath the weight of the silence. She mentally reviewed her lesson plans for her adult education class. She went over her list of items to pack for the weekend, deciding she'd better add a good book or two. She certainly couldn't count on Mac's scintillating conversation to keep her stimulated.

Mac suddenly looked up from his dinner and flushed. "I apologize," he said, pushing his plate away. "I'm so accustomed to eating alone, I guess

I've forgotten how to make interesting dinner conversation."

Abby felt a blush stain her own cheeks. Was it possible he could read minds? "It's all right," she said quickly. "I was just going over my lesson plans for my class."

"It must be rewarding to teach adult education," he observed.

She nodded. "It is. Adults are in the class because they want to be, not because they have to be. For the most part they're highly motivated and want to make positive changes in their lives." She paused a moment, took a sip of her tea, then continued. "I guess your job is a lot like mine."

"How so?" His dark brows shot up quizzically.

"You give sentences, hoping that those convicted will learn a lesson and go on to better things. I teach, hoping for the same results." Abby paused a moment, looking into Mac's ash-colored eyes. "I'm glad you didn't jail the woman for shoplifting."

Mac folded his hands in front of him and leaned his chin on them, his gaze thoughtful. "I hope it was a sound decision. So much of what I do has to depend on gut instinct."

"Is your gut instinct ever wrong?"

"Rarely." He looked at his watch. "I hate to cut this short, but it's time for me to get back to the courthouse."

Abby nodded and stood up, aware that it was time for her to leave for her class, as well. Mac got up and signaled to Cindy for their check. When it came they walked toward the cash register at the front of the coffee shop. Abby pulled some bills out of her purse and handed them to him. When he started to protest, she cut him short. "Mac, this was a meeting, not a date. I told you before, I pay my own way."

He hesitated a moment then nodded, took the money from her and paid the cashier.

The early autumn night air was cool as they left the coffee shop. Abby wrapped her arms around herself, wishing she'd remembered to bring a sweater with her. She'd have to be sure and pack warm clothes for the weekend. "We're all set for Friday then?" she asked.

"I think so. If you think of anything else we need to discuss, feel free to call me." They stopped in front of the courthouse.

"I will, but I think we have everything settled. I'll see you on Friday."

"I'm looking forward to it," he answered, but the words sounded like empty platitudes to Abby. That was fine with her. She wasn't jumping up and down with eager anticipation about the weekend, either.

"Come on, Charley, we're going to be late and you know how upset Harry gets when we aren't there on time," Abby called out from the front door.

"Just a second," Charley yelled from her bedroom.

Abby sighed and looked at her watch. Ten until six. Harry had said he'd be serving dinner promptly at six. "Come on, Charley. You know Harry will pout if we're late and spoil his dinner."

"I'm coming, I'm coming," Charley answered, emerging from the bedroom. In her hand she held her Walkman portable stereo, and as Abby waited impatiently, Charley replaced the old batteries with new ones. "This is my defense against Harry," she explained. "If he starts talking to me like I'm a big baby, I'll just plug into my music and ignore him."

"Now don't be rude to him," Abby admonished as they walked out of the apartment and toward their car. "You know Harry loves you like a daughter. He's been good to both of us through the years."

"Yeah, I know. And I really do love Harry. He just makes me crazy sometimes." Together they got into the car and headed for Harry's apartment on the other side of town. "I can't wait until tomorrow night," Charley exclaimed, her brown eyes gleaming with excitement. "What time are they supposed to pick us up?"

"Five. You make sure you come right home after school so you can pack your clothes," Abby instructed. "And don't forget to put in that brown sweater."

"Ah, Mom, that's so ugly," Charley protested.

"But it's warm. Besides, who's going to see you?"

"I guess that's true," Charley agreed. "The weatherman this morning said this may be our last nice weekend of Indian summer, then rain is moving in."

"I just hope it holds off until after our camping trip," Abby said with a frown. The only thing that could make the weekend plans more abhorrent would be a downpour of rain.

"Don't forget to get marshmallows. Lauren and I want to roast them over the fire. And we want to have a sing-along and tell ghost stories and take nature walks and catch fish." Charley paused to catch her breath.

Abby laughed at her daughter's enthusiasm. Despite the fact that she was dreading the weekend, she didn't want to dampen Charley's exuberance. "I'm sure you'll have a great time," she replied.

"But Lauren and I want you and Judge Stewart to have fun, too," Charley added.

"Oh, I'm sure we will," Abby returned smoothly, although she was certain of no such thing.

Mac had been on her mind the past two nights, ever since their meeting in the coffee shop. She found herself wondering about his wife. What kind of a woman would have married such a taciturn man? And what had caused the breakup of their marriage? Perhaps he'd bored her into divorce court. She smiled at this thought. The smile lasted only a moment, then faded.

He'd surprised her that night. As she'd sat in the back of the courtroom waiting for the evening recess, she'd been struck by how cold, how merciless he'd looked. Yet, when compassion was needed, he'd shown compassion.

Perhaps there was more to the man than met the eye. Maybe he was like an artichoke. You had to get through layers of tough skin before you reached the meat of the man. She scoffed at these thoughts. The last thing she needed in her life was a judgmental, unsociable, ill-natured man. She didn't need anyone in her life except Charley and good old Harry.

She pulled into Harry's apartment-complex parking lot, dismissing all thoughts of Mac Stewart from her mind.

"It's about time," Harry greeted them at the door. "Another five minutes and the lasagna would be burned and the bread dried out."

"Good evening to you, too," Abby said, giving the little man a fond kiss on the cheek.

"Come in." Harry ushered them inside. "It's ready right now, so why don't you go ahead and sit down."

Abby and Charley went into the dining room and sat down at the exquisitely set table while Harry hurried back into the kitchen. Abby always loved to have dinner with Harry because he never did anything halfway. His meals were not only exercises in gourmet cooking, but aesthetic pleasures, as well.

The smoked-glass dining table was set with white and black dishes. Red napkins fanfolded added a dash of bold color. Red wine chilled in a silver ice bucket, and the centerpiece, a dozen red roses artfully arranged in a silver vase, added its elegance and scent to the surroundings.

"Is there anything I can do to help?" Abby offered, already knowing the answer.

"Absolutely not," Harry replied, emerging from the kitchen carrying a dish of vegetable lasagna. "Just let me get the salad and the bread and we're all ready."

Minutes later they all sat together at the table, enjoying the wonderful meal and an easy exchange of pleasantries. Even Charley cooperated, groaning only once when Harry leaned over and pinched her cheek with affection. The talk revolved around their work. Harry entertained them with courtroom dramas and Abby spoke about her days at school.

"Harry, did Mom tell you we're going camping this weekend?" Charley asked when there was a lull in the conversation.

Harry looked at Abby incredulously. "Camping? You?" He laughed as if it was the funniest thing he'd ever heard.

"What's so funny?" Abby demanded.

Harry wiped his mouth with his napkin, but was unsuccessful at wiping the grin off his face. "I'm sorry, I just can't imagine you roughing it. You're a creature of comfort, Abby. Why on earth are you going camping?"

Abby's mouth worked, but no logical reason fell out.

"She's going because Judge Stewart said she wouldn't," Charley said with a giggle.

Harry's eyes grew huge in his face. "Judge Stewart? Judge Eldridge Stewart... Stoneface?"

"The very same," Abby replied with a grim smile. She quickly told him the circumstances that led up to the trip.

"You and Judge Stewart on a camping trip..." Harry shook his head and laughed once again. "It's sort of like the Pope and Madonna going rafting."

"I'm not like Madonna," Abby protested.

"You know what I mean," Harry insisted. "You're outgoing and love having fun. You're impulsive and people-oriented. Judge Stewart is nothing like that."

"Honestly, Harry. It's just a dumb camping trip." Abby shoved her plate away. "This meal was wonderful. You're going to make somebody a fine wife someday," she teased, more to change the subject than anything else.

"Actually, that's why I invited you over here this evening. I have an announcement to make." He paused a moment, a blush moving across his face, not stopping until it had engulfed even the tips of his ears. "I'm getting married."

"What?" Abby and Charley both looked at him incredulously. "But I didn't even know you were seeing anyone in particular," Abby said.

"We sort of kept it quiet," he explained. "Her name is Kathleen Winters and she's a law clerk down at the courthouse."

"But you've always said that you're a die-hard bachelor," Charley declared.

"So I did," he agreed. "But I didn't expect to find somebody like Kathleen. I didn't count on Cupid's potent arrow shooting me right in the heart."

"Tell me about her," Abby prompted, still shocked by his announcement.

"She's a widow. She has two grown children and she's absolutely wonderful." There was a look in his eyes she'd never seen before, a look she envied because she knew it was love.

She reached over and clasped his hand in hers. "Harry, I'm so happy for you."

Charley excused herself from the table and went into the living room, obviously bored with the adults' conversation.

"When's the wedding?" Abby asked.

"We're planning a Christmas ceremony. We haven't pinned down a specific date yet." He paused to pour them each more wine. "It will be a small ceremony, just family and close friends. Of course I want you and Charley there." He laughed self-consciously. "Imagine this all happening now, at my age. It's crazy."

"But it's a wonderful kind of crazy." Abby smiled at him and squeezed his hand once again. "Come on, let's get these dishes cleaned up and while we do you can tell me how you met this wonderful Kathleen and how she stole your heart."

Lucky, lucky Harry, Abby thought later as she and Charley drove back home. He'd finally found love and Abby was thrilled for him.

As they'd washed the dishes and cleaned up the kitchen, Harry had talked about Kathleen, telling Abby how he'd met her almost a year ago and how they'd been seeing each other on a regular basis. As he talked about her, his voice reflected his deep emotion for the woman.

Abby was happy for Harry. She'd always known that he would make someone a wonderful husband and had often wished he'd find love. Yes, she was happy for him, but she also knew that his relationship with Kathleen would be the end of his relationship with Abby. Of course Harry wasn't aware that his marriage would change things, but Abby was a realist. She knew no woman, no matter how nice, would want a divorced woman and her teenage daughter hanging around, intruding in Harry's life. And Abby wouldn't want to intrude.

She turned into her parking space, turned off her engine and sighed, suddenly overwhelmed with an aching loneliness.

Chapter Six

"They're here? They're here!" Charley flew out the door after screaming her announcement of Mac and Lauren's arrival.

Abby looked at her watch. Exactly five o'clock. Somehow she wasn't surprised by Mac's to-the-minute promptness.

She stepped over the pile of camping equipment that was stacked just inside the apartment and opened the door to greet them.

"All ready?" Mac asked, stepping through the doorway and eyeing her pile.

Abby nodded, struck dumb for a moment by his appearance. He'd left his tailored suit and tie behind. He wore a pair of jeans that molded lovingly to the length of his legs. A bulky-knit gray sweater hugged his broad shoulders and emphasized the flatness of his stomach. His hair looked different, more tousled and windblown. He looked younger, more vital and alive. He looks...fantastic, Abby thought, disturbed by this new dimension to him.

"Abby?" He looked at her questioningly.

She blushed, aware that she'd been staring. "I'm sorry, what did you say?"

"Are you ready to go?" he asked, his expression still quizzical.

"Of course I'm ready. You did say five o'clock." She busied herself buttoning up her cardigan. As a judge he seemed distant and unreachable, but in these clothes he was overwhelmingly masculine, and it was this change that threw her for a loop.

"I'll just get these things loaded," he said, picking up the tent and a large duffel bag.

Abby nodded, grabbed a small suitcase and followed him out.

"You girls can get the rest of the stuff," Mac instructed Lauren and Charley as he opened the trunk of his car.

The girls ran inside for the rest of the gear and Mac leaned over the bumper of the car, rearranging his equipment to make room for hers.

As he stretched, Abby admired the way his jeans molded to his lean buttocks. As Charley and her friends would say, the man had great buns. She'd always admired cute buns on a man and Mac was definitely a winner in that category.

"Mom?" Abby whirled around and saw Charley and Lauren lugging a large cooler. "Where should we put this?"

"I'll take it," Mac said, hefting the cooler out of the girls' hands.

Abby covered her cheeks with her hands, wondering if her blush was as obvious on the outside as it was on the inside. *What's wrong with me?* she wondered. She'd been standing here staring at a man's rear end like some addlepated, sex-starved female.

"Abby?"

"Mom!"

She suddenly became aware of three pairs of eyes staring at her and realized some answer or comment was expected, but she had no idea what the question had been.

"Is that everything?" Mac asked, a tinge of irritation in his voice.

She quickly scanned the contents of the trunk and nodded.

Minutes later they were on their way. *I must have been crazy when I agreed to this,* Mac thought as he pulled out of her apartment parking lot and headed for the highway that would take them to their destination.

The thing that irked him the most was that it had been foolish masculine pride that had prompted him to agree. It had been his desire to prove both his daughter and Abby wrong about him. He was not a dull bore with his nose glued to a law book. But now he was stuck doing something he hated for a whole weekend with a woman he hardly knew and two giggling teenagers.

He could hear Lauren and Charley whispering in the back seat while Abby sat staring out the passenger window.

Even though Mac was not pleased with the circumstances that had brought them together now... even though he dreaded the idea of camping for two days, he was committed to proving that there was more to him than dusty old law books.

Despite the fact that he couldn't remember the last time he'd actively sought to socialize with a woman, the silence between him and Abby pressed on him and he decided to start a conversation now. Surely the weekend would be much more pleasant if he and Abby could find some common ground.

"Would you like to listen to some music?" he asked, gesturing to the car radio.

"If my choices are classical music or silence, I'll take the silence," she answered with a smile.

"How about a compromise, some light rock." Mac turned on the radio and tuned it to an easy-listening station.

"That's nice," Abby said as the mellow sounds of Dan Fogelberg filled the car.

"Are you from Baldwin originally?" Mac asked, surprised to discover that he was curious about her. *It's only natural to be curious,* he rationalized to himself. After all, they were going to spend the next two days together in relative isolation.

"Actually, I grew up in Indianapolis. I moved to Baldwin when I got married. My husband was transferred here and I quickly grew to love it. What about you?" she asked, returning his question.

"Baldwin born and raised. When the divorce was finalized I thought about picking up and leaving, beginning fresh in a new place. But Lauren's roots are here and I didn't think it would be fair to her."

In all the time she'd known him, this was the longest, most personal sentence she'd heard from him. "I felt the same way when I got divorced," she said, wanting to give him something of equal value in return. "I thought about moving back to Indianapolis, starting anew, but I realized I liked Baldwin, and more importantly, Charley liked it. So we stayed."

"Does your ex-husband still live in town?" Mac asked, turning the volume of the radio down a tad.

"No. He moved to Chicago and owns an insurance company there. We've managed to keep everything pretty friendly, and he sees Charley several times a year." She hesitated a moment. "What about your ex?"

"I don't know where she is and Lauren never sees her." His reply was brusque, his voice tense as he answered, and he immediately turned up the volume of the radio, making further conversation nearly impossible.

Uh-oh, Abby thought. She'd overstepped, apparently probed a tender area. She sighed and looked out at the passing scenery. Okay, now she knew that his divorce—or rather, his ex-wife—was a sore subject. Was it because he was still in love with her?

She looked back at him, noting how the shafts of sunlight radiating through the window found each silver strand in his hair and made it sparkle like Christmas tinsel on a tree. Had his heart been broken when his marriage had fallen apart? He didn't strike her as a man with a broken heart—rather, she decided he was a man without a heart.

She stole another glance at him, trying to imagine what his chest looked like without the concealment of the bulky sweater. She was certain it was nicely muscled, but if she leaned her head against it and thumped with her fist, she felt it would echo hollowly. Like the tin man in the classic movie, Mac had an empty chest. She sighed and refocused on the scenery outside the window.

"Shouldn't we be there by now?" Lauren asked some time later, leaning up over the front seat.

"As soon as we get there can we make a camp fire and roast marshmallows?" Charley asked, also leaning forward.

"The first thing we'll have to do when we arrive is set up our tents," Mac explained. Abby stifled a groan at the thought of wrestling with the contraption that would serve as their shelter for the next two nights. "After that we'll have to gather firewood and complete our campsite preparations. It will probably be a good hour before we'll be ready to toast marshmallows."

Abby looked at Mac in surprise. He certainly didn't come across as the Daniel Boone type, but he seemed to know what he was talking about. Again she was struck by the fact that there might be more to him than met her eye.

Her thoughts were interrupted by shouts of excitement from the girls. Ahead a sign read Lake Jackson 10 miles, and a large arrow pointed down a gravel road.

Mac made the turn and a short distance ahead they found the road bordered by thick woods whose trees were laden with autumn-colored leaves.

"Oh, it's beautiful," Abby said, opening her window a bit to allow the tangy scent of fall to enter.

"This is my favorite time of year," Mac observed.

"Not me. I'm a summer freak. I love hot summer nights and cold lemonade." Again she was struck by how different the two of them were. He liked classical music; she liked old rock and roll. He liked fall; she liked summer. If not for the friendship of their daughters, they would have absolutely nothing in common.

Within minutes they came to the camping grounds. After driving to several locations they came to a site a mere stone's throw from the edge of the lake. It was here that they decided to pitch camp.

It took several minutes to unload their equipment. Tents and coolers, sleeping bags and clothes, and finally the trunk of the car was empty.

"You need any help getting up your tent?" Mac asked.

Abby shook her head. "I'm sure Charley and I can manage just fine." She didn't want him to think she wasn't "wholesome" enough to know how to set up a tent. Besides, how difficult could it be?

Abby and Charley spread the tent out on the ground, a frown furrowing Abby's brow as she studied the piece of canvas and a handful of shiny silver poles. She saw how it was supposed to work, but as she quickly discovered, seeing and doing were two different things. She'd get one pole up only to have the other one fall down. As she worked, she was aware of Lauren and Mac's tent going up easily.

"Mom, we must be doing something wrong," Charley whispered.

"We'll get it," she grumbled. "Just hold that pole and don't let it fall." She was still muttering curses and battling the falling poles when Mac's tent was finished.

"Need some help?" he asked again, a small smile lifting one corner of his lips.

"I guess it's been a long enough time that I've sort of forgotten how to do it," Abby muttered, glancing over to Charley and Lauren who were crawling in and out of his domelike structure. "It sure didn't take you long to get yours up."

"I think I have an easier model than yours," he answered, grabbing a handful of the short lengths of rope that she hadn't known what to do with. "And I think it would help if you'd use these tie-downs." With his assistance it took only a few minutes to erect the tent. Abby thanked him, irritated that she'd required his help at all.

She spent the next few minutes laying out the sleeping bags and getting the rest of the equipment stowed away. Once this was done they decided to forage in the woods for firewood. Charley and Lauren grabbed hands and took off down a slightly overgrown path.

"Don't go too far and stay together," Mac yelled after them.

"I don't think you have to worry about them staying together," Abby observed wryly. "They've become pretty inseparable over the past couple of weeks."

"I imagine they'll do more giggling than gathering. I think I'll go get some firewood myself."

Abby watched him disappear down a path, irked by the fact he hadn't invited her to accompany him. *I didn't want to go with him anyway,* she thought perversely.

She walked over to several large dead tree trunks that were arranged around an old fire site. She checked, saw no creepy crawlers, and sat down.

Even though she hated camping, she couldn't help but admire the scenery that surrounded her. The sun sank slowly, casting its last lingering rays on the lake's surface, which shimmered with gold. The nearby trees whispered softly with the slight breeze that stirred the autumn leaves.

Abby wrapped her arms around herself, suddenly chilled. It would grow dark soon, and the night would turn even cooler. She looked at the path where Mac had disappeared, wishing he would hurry back. She suddenly felt alone...lonely, and she supposed his company was better than none at all.

She rose from the log where she'd been sitting, deciding she needed some activity while she waited. There were a lot of dead leaves and small twigs and sticks lying around their campsite. Maybe she could get a fire started before the others returned. She smiled at the idea. Wouldn't Mac be surprised!

She busied herself gathering what she thought would make good starter wood and bunches of dried leaves. She carefully arranged them all and pulled a pack of matches from her pocket. "A good scout is always prepared," she muttered, thankful that Becky had listed all the things that were "musts" on camping treks. Matches had been at the top of the list. It took only a moment or two for the dried leaves to catch fire and another few seconds for the twigs to burst into flames. Abby smiled in satisfaction, adding more leaves and twigs to keep the fire burning.

She frowned, realizing that if she was going to keep it going, she needed bigger pieces of wood. She paused a moment, listening for sounds of the girls or Mac returning, but the silence of the woods surrounded her.

She went over to the tent and pulled out the survival knife Becky had insisted she bring. Finding a pine tree with low, wrist-width branches, she used the serrated edge of the knife to saw one off. Working arduously, she cut the branch into several pieces and placed them on her fire, pleased as they popped and oozed and smoked... and smoked...

She coughed as the smoke rose thick and pungent, burning her eyes and forcing her backward. It poured off the fire, chasing her even farther away. She could feel the soot on her face, smell the acrid scent lingering in her hair.

"Abby, are you all right?" Mac came running up the path. He moved swiftly over to the fire and kicked off the branches she'd placed on it.

"What are you doing?" Abby asked irritably, watching as he destroyed her fire with his feet. "You're ruining my fire!"

"This isn't a fire," he replied tersely. "This is an ancient form of communication... smoke signals." He stamped out the last of the smoldering wood and confronted her. "What were you trying to do? Asphyxiate us all?"

"I was trying to start a fire," Abby retorted. "Who do you think you are, Smoky the Bear?"

For a moment they both glared at each other, then the left corner of Mac's lips quirked upward. "I'm not hairy enough to be Smoky."

"You ruined my fire," Abby said, trying to hang on to her irritation at his high-handed actions.

"It needed to be ruined. You must have used green wood." He smiled.

Abby found her breath caught in her throat. It was the smile she'd envisioned, one of warmth and promise, and her anger evaporated like mist in the sunlight. "I...it was silly of me to use green wood," she stuttered, focusing her gaze on the remains of the fire and away from his evocative smile. "I... uh...just thought it would be nice if I could get the fire started before you got back. It was starting to cool off..." She let her voice trail off and looked back at him.

"No big deal," he replied, shrugging his broad shoulders. "We'll just start another one, this time with dry wood. I dropped some on the path when I saw all the smoke. I'll be right back." He disappeared again into the woods and Abby released a shaky sigh.

"Get a grip, Abby," she muttered to herself, gathering up more dried leaves. The man only smiled. But there was no way she could explain the reason why that smile had made her knees feel shaky. There was no reason for the sudden desire she had to feel that smile, those lips against her own.

It's the smoke, she thought. *I'm suffering hallucinations due to carbon monoxide poisoning.* She felt somewhat better with this thought in mind, and when Mac returned with an armload of wood, she smiled, confident her crazy emotions were back in order.

By the time they had a smokeless, blazing fire going, the girls returned. Lauren carried an armful of wood and Charley had her arms laden with a collection of rocks, plants and flowers that had captured their attention.

The evening went by quickly. They dined on hot dogs cooked over the fire. Twice Abby's fell off into the ashes. She pulled it out and brushed it off each time, but when it was ready to eat she'd lost her appetite.

The girls kept up a steady stream of chatter. As night fell, their voices rang hollowly through the clearing. Once they had finished eating, Charley and Lauren toasted marshmallows and their talk turned to ghost stories.

Abby sat on the ground and leaned back against the fallen log. Although her back was chilly, the fire warmed her front, making her face burn. She felt no inclination to join in the girls' conversation. She was content to just sit, stare into the fire and let the girls' voices waft over her.

So far the trip had been ten times worse than she'd anticipated. Her stomach rumbled with hunger and her hair and clothes smelled of noxious smoke. She was exhausted, but dreaded the thought of crawling into the sleeping bag in the tent. She wished with all her heart she was going home to her wonderfully soft, warm bed.

She looked over at Mac, who sat directly across the fire from her. His bold features were highlighted by the fire's glow. He stared into the flames as if mesmerized by some vision dancing there. He'd been quiet throughout the meal, and even now he seemed far removed from this moment in time. *He's probably reviewing some law decision,* she thought.

She wondered if he was sorry he'd come. Did he wish he was going home to his own bed? She couldn't quite see him snuggled into a soft mattress covered with quilts. He probably slept on a bed of nails. She smiled inwardly at this thought even though she knew she probably wasn't being fair in her assessment of him. But the more time she spent with him, the more she was convinced that the man was a cold fish. He seemed so emotionless, so devoid of even the most basic human feelings.

As she stared at him, he looked up suddenly, his eyes capturing hers. For a long moment their gazes remained locked and in the gray depths of his she saw something flicker, something indefinable. It was there only a moment, then gone. He stood up, stretching his arms over his head.

"I think I'll call it a night," he said, looking over at Lauren. "I don't want you up too late, Lauren. If we're going to do some fishing in the morning we need to get an early start."

"Okay," Lauren agreed.

"I think I'll call it a night, too." Abby rose as well, realizing she was exhausted. "And I agree with Mac. You girls shouldn't be up too much longer."

With murmured good-nights, Mac went to his tent and Abby to hers. Once inside, Abby lit the Coleman lantern, which cast dancing shadows all around the tent interior. The next thing she did was check the inside of their sleeping bags, making certain no unwanted "guests" had crawled in for the warmth. Then she began to change out of her clothes, anxious for the oblivion of sleep.

Mac sat just inside his tent, unwilling to lie down and sleep with the girls still up. His tent was far enough away that he couldn't distinguish what the girls were saying, but he enjoyed the sound of their voices, the pleasant ring of their laughter. He was glad he'd come, if for no other reason than Lauren was having fun. Lately he'd spent so much time at work, he'd neglected spending quality time with his daughter.

So far the trip had not been too unpleasant, although he found himself entertaining strange, unsettling thoughts about Abby. The first time was when he'd stomped out her fire and she'd called him

Smoky the Bear with her eyes blazing in anger. He'd had a sudden desire to drag her into his arms, hold her achingly close and fit her curvaceous body against his. It had been a fleeting thought, gone in an instant.

However, it had happened again only moments ago when their eyes had met across the fire's glow. He'd wanted to touch her, feel the warmth of her skin against his. Strange, he hadn't realized until that moment that he had been cold for the past three years, since the day Melinda had walked out of his life.

He leaned forward and looked over to Abby's tent, his chest tightening as he saw her silhouette cast on the outside of the tent canvas by the lantern within. She was changing clothes and he knew he should look away, but he couldn't. It was like watching a strange, erotic strip show as he saw her pull her sweater over her head, then step out of her jeans. The slender shapeliness of her body was perfectly displayed...the upward thrust of her breasts, the flatness of her stomach... She called up an emotion Mac didn't want, a desire he couldn't fight.

He breathed a sigh of relief as the lantern went out, leaving her tent in darkness. Yes, something strange was happening to him, and he didn't like it one bit. He crawled to his sleeping bag and climbed in, hoping that whatever it was, like a bad drunk, he would sleep it off.

* * *

"Lauren, what are we gonna do?" Charley whispered, moving closer to the fire. She looked first at Mac's tent, then at her mother's. "Nothing is happening between them, nothing at all."

"I know," Lauren replied dispiritedly, picking up a stick and poking the fire. "I thought sure that if we got them out here with nobody else around, something would happen."

"Maybe it's not meant for them to fall in love," Charley said.

"No, I still think they're perfect for each other," Lauren protested. "They're two lonely people and they belong together. My dad needs somebody fun like your mom. All we need to do is be a little patient."

Charley was silent for a moment. "I stink at being patient," she finally confessed.

"So do I," Lauren said with a giggle. "But I guess that's all we can do for right now. Grown-ups seem to do everything more slowly than us." She sighed. "Maybe tomorrow will be a better day."

"I sure hope so," Charley said fervently.

Chapter Seven

Somebody had beaten her all night long. That was Abby's first thought when she awakened the next morning. Every muscle in every part of her body ached. As in *The Princess and the Pea,* she'd felt every stone, every ridge in the ground beneath her all night long.

She stifled a moan as she sat up, wondering if it was possible to die from too much ground contact. She glared at her daughter, who was curled up in her sleeping bag peacefully asleep. Oh, to be young again and be able to sleep soundly no matter what the circumstances.

A bone popped audibly in her back as she rolled out of her sleeping bag and reached hurriedly for her clothes. The early morning air was nippy and Abby added a heavy sweater to her jeans and sweatshirt.

The sun just barely peeked over the horizon as she left the tent and walked out into the crisp new day. There was no movement from Lauren and Mac's tent. *They're probably sleeping peacefully,* she thought resentfully.

She stirred the glowing embers of the fire and added a handful of twigs to get it going again. As she waited for the fire to become hot enough to add a larger log, she wrapped her arms around herself and muttered a curse. She must have been out of her mind when she'd agreed to this madness. She was too old for such nonsense.

It was a good thing she'd been born in this century, for she certainly wouldn't have survived pioneer days. Harry had been right; she was a creature of comfort. And this definitely wasn't comfort.

With the fire blazing warmth, she poked around in the box of cooking utensils Becky had donated, coming up with a battered but serviceable coffeepot. Filling it with some of the bottled water they'd brought, she added coffee and placed it on the wire rack she set up over the fire.

As she waited for the coffee, she sat down on one of the logs. This was the last time... the very last time she would allow Charley to talk her into anything!

She stared out at the lake and rubbed her eyes tiredly. If anything, she was more exhausted this morning than she'd been last night. She'd had trouble getting to sleep the night before. She'd never known how noisy the woods could be, and each sound sent her imagination flying. A twig snapping became the signal of the approach of a marauding bear. A bullfrog's low-throated croak had become some strange, female-eating monster. She'd finally fallen asleep some time just before morning.

"Just let this weekend end and get me back to the city where I belong," she breathed tiredly.

Eyeing the placid lake sparkling in the early morning light, she decided maybe she'd feel better if she splashed cold water on her face. Besides, it would take a few minutes for the coffee to be ready.

She walked down to the shoreline, pleased to see there was a small ledge where she could kneel down and be right next to the water. She carefully maneuvered herself, perching precariously in the awkward position, noting that the water was clear and looked clean. She scooped up a handful and sluiced her face, the chill momentarily stealing her breath away. It was bracing, just what she needed to shrug off the remaining sloth from her sleep.

"Good morning."

The voice, so near to her, startled her. She jumped and tried to turn, but instantly knew with a sinking heart that she was dangerously off balance. Before this thought fully registered, she fell into the lake.

The water was only about a foot deep, but she floundered for a moment, unable to get her footing. Finally she pushed herself out and up, turning to glare at Mac who stood and stared at her in stunned surprise.

"Are...are you all right?" he asked, holding out a hand to help her.

"No, I'm not all right," Abby snapped, slapping away his hand as she stomped up to the shore. She instantly began to shiver uncontrollably. "W-W-W-Why did you have to s-s-sneak up on me like that?"

"I didn't mean to sneak up on you," he returned, his brow wrinkled in concern. "Come on, we'd better get you out of those cold, wet clothes." He took her arm and led her back to her tent. "Do you have some extra clothing to change into?"

She nodded, her teeth clattering together so violently she couldn't speak. She stumbled into the tent, pulling off the cold, wet clothing, wondering if she would ever get warm again.

"Mom, what are you doing?" Charley asked sleepily.

"I'm ch-ch-changing my c-c-c-clothes, what does it l-l-look like I'm d-d-doing," Abby stuttered.

"What happened?" Charley shoved her hair out of her eyes and sat up.

"I f-f-fell in the l-l-lake."

"What?" A little quirk of a smile appeared at the corner of Charley's mouth.

"Charlene Renee Jones, if you dare laugh at me, I promise you'll be grounded until you're thirty years old!" Abby snapped, the chills slowly receding as she finished changing into dry things.

Charley buried her head in the sleeping bag, but Abby could tell by her heaving backside that she was desperately trying to stifle a fit of giggles. This only made Abby's mood more black.

Abby stomped back outside. Mac motioned for her to sit on the log nearest the fire and he silently handed her a cup of hot coffee. The fire warmed her outside and the strong coffee worked on the inside. Within minutes, she felt better. She watched as Mac found an old cast-iron frying pan and filled it with bacon. He placed it on the rack over the fire and immediately the smell filled the clearing and caused a rumbling in Abby's stomach.

Mac kept his gaze averted from her, and Abby had a feeling it was because he, too, was having trouble suppressing his amusement. "Go ahead and laugh," she finally said. "If my own daughter laughed at my misfortune, why shouldn't you?"

Mac looked at her, his gray eyes warm and crinkling at the corners with his smile. "I never laugh at other people's misfortunes, but you did look pretty funny."

Abby grinned, realizing there was no reason to be angry with him. He'd merely said good-morning. He'd had no idea he'd surprise her into falling in the lake. "I guess I did," she agreed.

"Are you warm now? You don't want to get sick."

She nodded, warmed more by the concern in his voice than anything else. "I'm fine. The fire feels good."

"How's the coffee?"

"Terrible," she answered truthfully. "But at least it's hot."

He turned back to the skillet and poked the bacon, which sizzled and popped ferociously. "I think I'm burning this," he muttered.

Abby set her cup down and went over to the skillet. "Here, let me see." She took the fork from him and prodded the blackened strips of meat. "Yeah, I'd say it's pretty burned. I guess cooking over a fire takes a particular talent."

"One I apparently don't have," Mac replied.

Abby smiled up at him. "Then we're in trouble, because I don't have it, either."

Breakfast was horrid. The coffee was too strong, the bacon was burned, and the eggs runny. They tried browning English muffins, but when the third one fell off the rack and into the fire, they decided to eat them straight out of the package, dry and cold.

After breakfast they all decided to try their hands at fishing. Mac provided the worms, having bought a couple dozen the day before just for this occasion. The girls found a spot down the lake, leaving Mac and Abby alone.

With a minimum of trouble Abby threw her bait-laden hook out into the water while Mac did the same. They stood side by side, close enough so she could smell his evocative scent, see the dark shadow of a morning stubble on his chin. He wore another sweater today, a blue one that made his gray eyes brighter. Again she noticed the way the worn jeans hugged his long legs, caressed his slender hips. Drat the man, anyway. It didn't seem fair that such attractiveness was wasted on him.

She turned and looked down the shore as she heard the girls squealing and laughing as they tried to bait their hooks.

"They're having fun," Mac observed.

"Yes, they are," Abby agreed, smiling as she watched Lauren chase Charley with a worm in her hand. "Lauren is such a pretty girl. She's going to be a real knockout someday," she said.

"I know," Mac replied glumly. "I think I'd like it better if she had warts on the end of her nose and a perpetual case of bad breath."

His humor, so unexpected and out of character made a burst of laughter bubble out of Abby. "I guess all parents feel that way when their daughters reach dating age."

"Lauren is far from dating age," Mac objected. "I'm not going to let her date for at least another two years."

Abby looked at him in surprise. "You'll be bucking the system. These days the girls are dating at fourteen. Of course Charley has a reasonable curfew and I have to meet the boy in question."

"Fourteen is too young to be dating," Mac said, his voice heavy with disapproval.

Abby opened her mouth to object, then shut it once again. Mac's opinions on dating were not her concern, and she wasn't about to fight with him over the topic.

She reeled up her line, checked her bait and swung the rod over her head to cast once again. She yelped in pain as the hook, instead of flying out into the water, tangled in the back of her hair.

Mac, hearing her yelp, instantly took in the situation. He dropped his pole and took hers, releasing enough line so he could lay it on the ground. "Hold still," he instructed her, turning her around so he stood just behind her.

Gently he parted her hair to find the tangled hook. The strands of her dark hair felt like watered silk as they caressed the back of his hands. He could smell the scent of it, that peach perfume he'd found so evocative when he'd danced with her at the school dance. Instantly, blood surged through his veins, pounding in a strange rhythm as a swift desire stole over him.

He could see the soft skin of her neck and he suppressed the need to place his lips there, make her gasp with pleasure and turn to offer him her lips.

Visions danced in his head, visions of her on a hot summer night wearing nothing but a necklace and sipping a cold glass of lemonade...the two of them moving together on sweat-slickened sheets while a summer breeze caressed their flesh.

Her body was warm against his and despite the chill of the day, he felt beads of perspiration break out across his forehead.

"Mac?"

Her voice jolted him out of his fantasies. "Yeah, I've just about got it," he said, his hands now trembling as they worked to remove the hook. "Done," he said, handing her the hook and grabbing up his own pole. "I think I'll try down the shore a little ways." He walked down the edge of the lake, away from Abby and the heat of her body.

For the rest of the morning, Mac kept his distance from her, afraid of the feelings she pulled out of him. The fishing produced no fish and within an hour the girls were ready for a hike.

They hiked through long-forgotten, overgrown trails, the girls in the lead. Mac followed next with Abby bringing up the rear. They walked until Mac's calves ached, reminding him that lately he'd neglected his workouts at the health club. Finally, the girls tired and they all went back to the camp for lunch.

After eating his fill of ham and cheese sandwiches, Mac decided to take a nap while the females collected wildflowers. As he lay alone in his tent, he contemplated his feelings for Abby. He couldn't ignore them any longer; he was definitely sexually attracted to the woman. It was the first time he'd felt such a thing since his divorce.

Surely it's a healthy sign, he rationalized. Surely it meant he'd finally put the past behind and was ready to begin living again. So what happened now? Did he act on his desire? He had Lauren's relationship with Charley to consider. He wouldn't want to do anything to jeopardize the girls' friendship. Where did he go from here?

He sighed. Lord, he was tired. He hadn't slept much at all last night. Maybe if he took a little nap, his confusion about Abby would become less perplexing. He closed his eyes....

"Gosh, I'm really tired," Lauren moaned, stretching her arms over her head and stifling a yawn. "I think I'll go to bed."

"But it's so early," Abby protested. They had just finished eating dinner and the sun was now disappearing beneath the horizon.

"It must be all this fresh air and exercise, 'cause I'm pooped, too," Charley added. "I think I'll hit the old sleeping bag, as well."

Together the two girls said good-night and disappeared into their respective tents. Abby and Mac remained at the fire.

"Are you tired?" he asked her, getting up to pour himself another cup of coffee from the pot warming by the fire.

"Not really," Abby answered. She was, but she certainly wasn't looking forward to another night on the hard ground. Besides, the crackling fire was pleasant and the stars overhead formed a balcony of diamonds.

"Coffee?"

She nodded and handed him her cup. He poured the coffee then joined her on the log. For a few minutes they sat quietly, sipping their drinks and listening to the sounds of night that surrounded them. Unlike the earlier uncomfortable silences between them, this one was different, pleasant.

"I never realized how noisy the woods are," Abby observed after a few minutes.

"I noticed last night. I thought I'd never get to sleep."

She looked at him in surprise, then smiled. "I had trouble getting to sleep, too." She looked toward the lake. "There's a bullfrog down there who croaked all night long."

Mac nodded his head. "When I finally did go to sleep, I dreamed of frying frog legs all night long."

Abby laughed, again pleased at his sense of humor. "Personally, I could go for a fat, greasy hamburger right about now."

"Hmm, dripping with ketchup and mustard and heaped with pickles and onions," Mac added, smiling at her. "The steaks were pretty bad, weren't they?"

Abby grinned. "Not at all. I always like burnt shoe leather for supper." She sighed and sipped her coffee.

"The fire is nice, isn't it?"

"Hmm." Abby nodded, staring into the flickering flames. "I suppose everyone who looks into one sees something different."

"I see a fat, greasy hamburger dripping with ketchup and mustard," he replied dryly.

Abby laughed and in that moment she realized that at some point during the course of the day she'd begun to like him. She sighed again and looked at him tentatively. "I have a confession to make," she said hesitantly.

"What?" He looked at her curiously.

"I hate camping." Now that the truth was out, she felt a huge sense of relief. "I hate hiking and fishing and sleeping in a tent. I hate all of this."

"Then why did you come?" he asked incredulously.

"Because the girls told me you didn't think I would. They implied that you didn't think I was wholesome enough to enjoy outdoorsy kinds of things." She flushed. "I reacted childishly and agreed to come."

Mac stared at her for a long moment, then he began to laugh. It started out as a little chuckle, but quickly grew until he threw his head back and was laughing uproariously.

The sound of it made chills dance up and down Abby's arms. It was the most pleasant sound she'd ever heard. "What's so funny?" she asked, wishing he would laugh forever. She leaned toward him, pulled closer by the magnetism of his laughter.

Mac caught his breath, a boyish grin on his face. "Oh, Abby, I think we've been had."

"What do you mean?"

"I was told that you thought I wouldn't come because I'd rather have my nose stuck in a law book."

"I never said any such thing!" Abby protested.

"And I never said anything about you. To tell the truth, I've only been camping once in my life and I hated it. I still hate it."

Abby looked at him in surprise. "But you seem quite adept—I mean, you put your tent up so easily and you knew just what had to be done."

Mac grinned sheepishly. "Now I have a confession to make. I bought the tent last week and practiced putting it up every night in my living room. It took me three hours the first time."

Abby shook her head ruefully. "What a pair we are. I'm not sure who deserves to be punished more, the girls for cooking up this scheme or us for behaving like children."

"I think we've been punished enough," Mac replied. "There isn't a muscle in my body that isn't hurting tonight."

"I can definitely relate to that," Abby agreed.

Mac shook his head and stared into the fire reflectively. "Actually, I'm glad the girls weaseled us into coming here."

"Why?" Abby asked in surprise.

He looked at her, his features softened by the fire's glow and his inner thoughts. "Lauren's been after me for months to start dating, to get on with my life. Did you find it hard to start dating again after your divorce?"

Abby stared into the blaze, trying to think back to that time. "Yes, I think it's always difficult to close a chapter of your life and move on to the next."

Mac nodded, as if he'd expected her answer. "When Melinda left me, I was devastated. It was totally unexpected. As far as I was concerned, we had the perfect life together. My career was really taking off, we lived in a beautiful home, and we had Lauren." He paused a moment, his gaze back on the flames. "I didn't realize she was sneaking around behind my back, seeing other men, having affairs."

Pain was evident in his voice and Abby reached out to place her hand on his arm. He smiled absently at her gesture and continued. "When she told me she wanted a divorce and was moving in with another man, I was shocked, hurt, bewildered. She moved out and left Lauren with me, said she wanted to get settled, then would have Lauren join her. Lauren refused." He sighed tremulously. "It took both Lauren and me a while to recover." He smiled at her, a gesture that didn't quite hide the pain of his memories, his wife's betrayal.

Abby suddenly realized that Mac was not a man without emotions. He was a man as deep as the ocean, so deep, so full of feeling, that he had to control it with an ironclad will. She found herself leaning into him, an irresistible attraction pulling her toward him as she realized that his gruff exterior masked a vulnerable spirit.

"I think it's past time that I close a chapter and move on to the next one," Mac said, his body suddenly very close to hers.

She looked into the gray of his eyes and knew the painful memories of the past were gone, swallowed by a different emotion that radiated from the smoke of his eyes. In the space of a moment the mood between them changed, filled with tension, making Abby's breath shallow as anticipation and excitement raced through her.

He's going to kiss me, she thought. She could see the intention in his eyes. And what amazed her the most was how badly she wanted him to.

"Abby..." He breathed her name softly, then his lips moved to cover hers.

At first his kiss was soft, a tentative exploring. Then, with a moan, he wrapped his arms around her, pulling her against him, the kiss deepening in intimacy.

Abby lost herself in his embrace, reveling in the taste of him, the scent of him, the feel of his shoulder muscles beneath her hands.

When he finally released her, she drew a tremulous sigh, surprised at how intensely she'd responded to him.

"Maybe the girls aren't all wrong," he observed, a hand still on her back, moving in light circles of sensation.

"What do you mean?" she asked, afraid he would kiss her again... afraid that he wouldn't.

"About us." His hand on her back moved up into her hair where he caressed the nape of her neck. "Maybe they know something we don't know and we should just ride with it and see what happens."

"What do you have in mind?"

"How about having dinner together one night next week, just you and me?"

Abby nodded. "I'd like that. As long as it doesn't involve fresh air or open flames."

Mac laughed. "I promise."

"I think on that note I'll go to bed," Abby said, rising from the log as he did the same. She needed some time alone to think about the change in their relationship. It had happened so suddenly, and she found it not only confusing but exciting, as well.

Together they walked toward the tents. "Good night," she said, turning toward hers. He caught her arm and whirled her around, pulling her up against him.

"Good night," he whispered just before he delivered another toe-curling kiss.

Neither of the adults noticed the two girls peeking out between the flaps of the tents, grins of triumph on their faces.

Chapter Eight

"Come on, Mom. Mac's going to be here any time." Charley knocked impatiently on Abby's bedroom door. "You better hurry up. You don't want to be late for your date." She giggled.

"I'm just about ready," Abby answered, taking one last look in the mirror. She couldn't remember the last time she'd been so nervous before a date.

She hadn't seen Mac since they'd come back from the camping trip on Sunday, although in the last week she had talked to him twice on the phone. Both calls had been brief, a finalizing of their dinner date for tonight.

Abby had dressed with care, knowing the restaurant he'd chosen to take her to was luxurious. Her black dress was simple, yet classy, the red earrings and necklace adding a dash of bold color. She checked her refection again, then liberally spritzed herself with her favorite perfume.

"Mom, Mac's here." Charley beat a tattoo on her door.

Abby checked her watch, smiling at Mac's punctuality. Taking a deep breath, she left the bedroom and walked into the living room to greet him.

He stood just inside the door, looking as stiff and nervous as she felt. She gazed at him tentatively, worried suddenly that this was a horrid mistake. They'd let the moonlight at the campground and their kisses get to them. They'd been foolish to make a date. Then he smiled and suddenly everything was all right.

"You look lovely," he said, moving to help her on with her coat.

"Thanks. You don't look half bad yourself," she said teasingly. Actually, he looked terrific. Dressed in charcoal-colored slacks and a black dress shirt, he looked casually elegant.

"Come on, let's go!" Charley said impatiently.

The three of them got into Mac's car. The plan was to drop Charley off at his place where she and Lauren could spend the evening while Abby and Mac went out.

"I see you survived last weekend," he said as he pulled out of the parking lot.

Abby smiled. "It took a three-hour bath to soak out all the kinks."

"I spent about that same amount of time in my health club's sauna."

"You belong to a health club?" Abby asked curiously. Although he certainly looked to be in wonderful shape, he didn't seem the type to spend a lot of time working with weights or playing handball.

He nodded. "Although it's obvious I don't spend enough time there—otherwise I wouldn't have been so sore from the hiking."

"I gave Becky back all the camping equipment and told her if I ever came to borrow it again to get a straitjacket and put me in it."

Mac laughed, the pleasant rumble that made Abby's insides warm. "I sold mine to a secondhand sports equipment store. I promised them I wouldn't be back for it."

"I know I'll never go camping again."

"That's one thing we definitely agree on," he returned. He looked in the rearview mirror at Charley. "Lauren knows all the rules of staying home alone," he told her as they pulled up in front of his house.

The minute the car hit the driveway Lauren flew out the front door. "Come on, Charley, Dad said we could order pizza so I already called and got us a pepperoni and I checked out two awesome movies for us to watch on the VCR and we're going to have so much fun." Lauren paused to get a breath as Charley climbed out of the car.

"You two go and have fun. Don't worry about us," Charley urged, linking arms with her best friend.

"Yeah, stay out as late as you want," Lauren said with a giggle. The giggle was contagious and Charley joined her, both girls looking at Mac and Abby.

"Get in the house and make sure you lock the door," Mac instructed, then with a wave he backed the car out of the driveway, and he and Abby were on their way.

"Have you ever eaten at the Brass Gull?" he asked.

Abby shook her head. "It's been on my list of places to try, but I've never gotten around to it. I've heard wonderful things about it."

"The atmosphere is nice and the food is terrific, if you like seafood."

"Love it," Abby said agreeably. She settled back in the seat enjoying the easy conversation as they talked about favorite restaurants and foods. Finally they'd found something they had in common—they both enjoyed good food.

"Amigos has the greatest Mexican food," Abby said, their conversation continuing as they were led to a table in the elegant Brass Gull.

"Not true. Hombres over on Sixth Street is much better," Mac objected.

"I've never been there," she admitted, nodding her thanks to the waiter who seated her at the intimate table for two.

"We'll eat there next time," he replied. He slid into his seat and opened his menu.

Abby opened hers, as well, her heart flipping crazily at his words. Next time... that implied another date.

"How about a glass of white wine?" Mac asked as the waiter prepared to take their order. Abby nodded and Mac ordered a carafe of wine.

"This place is beautiful," Abby observed minutes later, sipping her wine and admiring the decor. The tables were small, each one set in a tiny alcove that provided maximum privacy. Green plants hung from brass pots, their vinery spilling down to embellish the intimate atmosphere.

"It is nice, isn't it," Mac agreed. "This is one of Lauren's favorite places to eat." He frowned suddenly.

"What's the matter?" Abby asked.

"Oh, it's just that Lauren and I seem to be going through a rocky period right now. She thinks I'm too strict," Mac explained.

Abby smiled. "Most teenagers think their parents are too strict."

"I just worry about her. I don't want her to make mistakes and I want her values to be sound."

Impulsively, Abby reached across the table and covered his hand with hers. She felt a tingle of pleasure as she came into contact with his warm skin. "The best you can hope for is that you give her a firm foundation so she can weather any storms on her horizon."

"I know one thing—" he smiled at her and turned his hand over to capture hers "—it's nice to share the worry with somebody who's experiencing the same things."

"You don't have any family? Any close friends you can turn to for support?" she asked, trying to ignore the way the warmth of his hand had crept up her arm, infusing her body with a welcomed heat.

He shook his head. "I don't have any family and I lost touch with Melinda's family at the time of the divorce."

"What about friends?"

"I realized after my wife left that our friends were actually her friends. Since then I've pretty well focused all my time and attention on my work."

His words conjured up the image of a solitary man, a man who knew loneliness, a man who had sought that state in an effort to heal the wounds left behind by his wife. And Abby was certain there were wounds, scars that lingered in the shadows of his eyes. "Haven't you heard the old saying? All work and no play makes Mac a dull man," she teased.

"Are you insinuating that you find me dull?"

"On the contrary, I find you rather fascinating," Abby said honestly, but with a light, teasing tone. "I've never known a judge before. I've always wondered what they wear under those long, black robes." She pulled her hand away from his in order to take another sip of her wine.

"I can't speak for all judges, but in my case I wear as little as possible."

Abby nodded with seeming nonchalance as her mind whirled with images of his lean, dark body beneath whispering black robes. It was an arousing vision, one that made a fire ignite in the pit of her stomach. She was grateful when the waiter appeared with their orders, dispelling the appealing fantasy.

As they ate, Mac noticed how the candlelight from the center of the table picked up the chestnut highlights in her dark hair. She was a sensual eater who savored each and every bite. Mac suspected she was a totally sensual woman who enjoyed the feel of silk against her skin, the taste of rich food, the sound of wind chimes dancing on a summer's breeze.

Apparently the wounds Melinda had left behind were scarring over. There had been a time when he'd thought they were lethal, but it appeared he would live, and he was ready to begin again with Abby. There was something about her that made him feel good. He hadn't realized that Melinda had stolen his laughter. But Abby with her wonderful sense of humor had given it back to him.

"How about more wine?" he asked, noticing she'd finished her first glass.

"Just half. One and a half glasses is my limit."

Mac grinned lazily. "I like a woman who knows her limitations." He poured more wine, surprised to realize he was flirting. And why not, he thought defiantly. Abby was an extremely attractive woman and he liked her.

Abby had a sudden feeling of danger, a sensation of treading water with no safe pool edge in sight. She knew he was flirting with her. What she hadn't realized was how vulnerable she would be to his attentions. She'd been flirted with before, but never had she felt this answering flutter in her stomach, the erratic pulse beat at the base of her throat. There was a heightened sense of excitement, a feeling of anticipation. His smoke-colored eyes held the hypnotic illumination of seduction, and what frightened and thrilled her was that she knew her eyes answered his call.

"How did you ever find this place? You're only the second or third person I've spoken to who's even heard of it," Abby asked, trying to find her footing, establish a neutral conversation to give herself time to adjust to the strange emotions he evoked.

"How did you hear about it?" he returned the question.

"My sister, Becky, and her family come here pretty often. Not only do they go camping on a regular basis, they also like to try new restaurants."

"Ah, too adventurous for my blood," Mac said. "Actually, I discovered this place while I was still in law school. I used to come here quite often myself. They have a small bar in the other room where a lot of lawyers hang out. A fellow student and I spent a lot of nights here unwinding."

"What happened to your friend? Did he become a judge, too?" Abby asked curiously.

"No, he dropped out of law school and moved to the West coast. Last I heard he was in California and had married some blond beach bunny."

"Ah, every man's fantasy." Abby laughed.

"No, not every man's fantasy," he countered. "Some men fantasize about dark-haired women who love hot summer nights and rock and roll music." The caress in his voice was as potent as a hand on her breast, a brush of lips against her thighs.

"Your Honor, you're out of order." She tapped the back of his hand lightly, her voice shaky.

"I demand a retrial," he responded, taking her hand in his and bringing it up against his lips.

Abby tried to think of a witty comeback, but the sensation of his warm, moist mouth against the back of her hand made coherent thought impossible. Could this be Stoneface Stewart, nibbling on her hand, making tingles of pleasure race up and down her spine?

She gently extricated her hand from his and focused on her plate, although her appetite for the scampi had diminished as another hunger grew.

"Abby?"

She looked at him, seeing an expression of embarrassment on his handsome face.

"I'm sorry if I pushed too hard. It's been a long time since I've pursued a relationship with a woman and I'm very much out of practice."

This confession, obviously difficult for him to make, only endeared him to her. Abby smiled gently, wanting to ease his discomfort. "I'm out of practice, as well," she admitted.

"But I want you to understand, I do want to pursue a relationship with you."

"I'm glad, but I think it's important we go slowly."

He nodded, and with this settled, a new, easy camaraderie sprang up between them as they finished the meal. He entertained her with stories from court and she told him about some of her favorite students. They laughed about the crazy circumstances that had first brought her to him as a defendant, then later as a "blind" date.

As they talked, Abby realized that something had happened to loosen him up, and she suspected it had been their conversation the week before at the campground. Since baring his heart and past, he seemed more comfortable with himself, more open and less like old "Stoneface."

"How did you ever get the nickname 'Mac' from Eldridge?" Abby asked when they'd finished the main course and were enjoying a cup of coffee.

"That happened in law school. My fellow classmates used to say I had all the tact of a Mack truck and so I became known as Mac." He grinned easily. "You have to admit, it beats going through life as an Eldridge."

"Eldridge does sound rather stuffy and somber. I definitely like you better as a Mac."

"Thank you," he said, his eyes twinkling warmly. "Now, how about some dessert? They have marvelous cheesecake here."

"Oh no, I couldn't eat another bite," she protested.

"When I get the check, I'm not going to have to fight with you, am I?" he teased. "After all, this was a real, official date."

Abby laughed. "Only if I can reciprocate and have you and Lauren eat dinner at my place tomorrow night." The invitation was impulsive, but the moment it fell out of her mouth she realized how much she wanted him to accept.

"You've got a deal," he agreed.

"Good," she said with a smile.

It was raining as they came out of the restaurant, a chilly, windblown storm. It seemed natural for Mac's hand to find hers, holding it with a grasp that was warm and welcome as they ran for the shelter of the car.

"Whew, where did this come from?" he exclaimed with a laugh, rubbing one hand over his wet hair and starting the engine with his other. Then he quickly reached for the heater controls.

"October wouldn't be complete without one of these blowing, chill-you-to-the-bones rains," she replied, shaking her head like a long-haired shaggy dog. "You're the one who said you loved the fall," she accused.

He nodded, looking wonderfully vital with his wind-whipped, rain-splattered hair. "And I do," he agreed, punching in a button that caused warm air to blow out of the vents.

As he drove back to his house, Abby found herself wondering if he would kiss her good-night. She hoped so. She'd spent the past week replaying his kiss at the campground. It had been an experience she definitely wanted repeated.

He parked the car in his driveway and shut off the engine. He unbuckled his seat belt and turned to look at her. "I love the sound of rain on the roof, don't you?" he observed, leaning toward her so that she felt the heat of his breath on her face. Again, she felt a stirring deep within her, the insistent fingers of desire stroking her from inside out. "It makes a sort of intimacy for the people who listen to it."

She opened her mouth, knowing some kind of answer was expected, but before one could escape, his lips touched hers. At first the touch was tentative, an experimental tasting, his lips the only point of contact between them. Yet as he deepened the kiss, she felt as if he was caressing her from head to toe.

The sound of the rain splattering on the car faded as her blood surged and her heart beat with a deafening rhythm. His mouth was hot and insistent and she felt the slight brushing of his whiskers against her chin. It was such an intimate, masculine kind of thing that it made her moan deep in the back of her throat.

His arms wrapped around her as he twisted in the seat, maneuvering her so he was half lying on top of her. His lips left hers only long enough to find the sensitive skin of her throat, where he rained tiny kisses that made Abby gasp with pleasure.

The intensity he displayed on the bench as a judge was there in his kiss as his lips once again engulfed hers, overwhelming her, demanding total capitulation. And she complied, answering him with demands of her own. She drank of him, her tongue first exploring, then retreating in a teasing game that had no rules.

She tasted as sweet as Mac had remembered from the week before. More sweet. Her lips were honey soft, drawing him back again and again for more of her nectar.

She smelled like an autumn night, all darkness and mystery, a mystery he wanted to fully investigate. Her body moved beneath his and the soft moan she emitted stirred his desire to a frenzy.

One of his hands tangled erotically in her hair as the other one moved between them, touching first the side of her breast, then covering the entire mound. Immediately he felt her nipple surging toward the heat of his hand as an answering tension circled in his groin,. He wanted her, here and now. He couldn't ever remember wanting a woman as badly as he wanted her. His lips touched her collarbone. He groaned in frustration as he encountered the barrier of her neckline.

Abby was lost in him, all reason gone as she gave herself to his touch, his caress. It was crazy, but she felt as if for the past ten years since her divorce, she'd been waiting for this moment with this man.

The atmosphere in the car grew more intimate as their breaths mingled together and steamed the windows. Mac couldn't get enough of her. He kissed her lips, her cheeks, her sweet-scented throat, finding the taste of her addictive. Her body was warm and soft beneath his, evoking in him a desire so intense he trembled. He shifted his position, wanting to get closer, instead cracking his hipbone on the steering wheel. He yelped and hissed a curse, and when he looked back at Abby he knew the mood had been broken.

She gently pushed against him, her blue eyes still darkened by passion. For a moment he resisted, wanting to continue, go on tasting her, feeling her. But he saw the desire ebb from her eyes and reluctantly smiled, touched her cheek lightly, then sat up and breathed a shaky sigh. "Have we lost our minds?" he asked after a moment.

"I think so," she answered, her voice as trembly as his. She laughed suddenly. "I'll tell you what's really crazy."

He looked at her curiously, still trying to get his desire under control. "What?"

"What's wrong with this picture?" she asked, laughter bubbling to her lips once again. "Here we are, two adults necking in the car while our children spy on us through the window." She pointed to the living-room window, where Lauren and Charley were peeking out.

Mac threw an arm around her shoulder and together they laughed, and in their shared laughter Mac had a sudden, strange thought. Was it possible he was falling in love with Abby Jones?

Chapter Nine

"That's it. We won the game," Charley announced proudly, adding up the scores of the card game they'd all been playing.

"That makes it tied. Dad, you and Abby won one and Charley and I won one. We've got to play the tiebreaker." Lauren grabbed the cards and began to shuffle.

Mac looked at his wristwatch and leaned back in his chair. "I hate to be a spoilsport, but it's getting pretty late and I've got court in the morning."

"Oh, Dad, don't be a party pooper," Lauren wailed, gazing at him pleadingly.

"Lauren, we don't want to overstay our welcome," Mac said, glancing over at Abby.

Abby smiled. "You don't have to worry about that," she assured him. "As far as I'm concerned, we can play cards all night. I don't have to be in court early in the morning."

"Come on, Dad. Just one more game," Lauren begged.

"Yeah, please. Just one more." Charley added her pleas to Lauren's.

"Okay, okay." Mac laughed in surrender. "I guess I'm outvoted. One more game," he agreed.

As they played the last game, Abby thought back over the evening. Mac and Lauren had arrived at six for Abby's spaghetti dinner. The spaghetti had been perfect, topped only by the easy conversation and pleasant company.

Mac had been in a wonderful mood from the moment they'd arrived. His smile appeared frequently, a special heat in his eyes each time they lingered on Abby. Abby knew he was remembering their kisses and caresses of the night before in his car. She'd had trouble forgetting them, as well. Her body had positively vibrated all night long with frustration, a state she hadn't been in for years.

She felt as if she were a teenager on a date, waiting for her parents to go to bed so she could make out with her date. Only this time there was no chance that the girls would leave them alone.

"Mom, it's your turn," Charley prompted, pulling Abby from her thoughts.

"Of course." Abby blushed, quickly throwing down a card. She immediately grimaced as she realized the card she'd thrown was one of the girls'. "Sorry," she apologized to Mac. Her blush deepened as Mac smiled at her, his eyes filled with a heat that seemed to spill out of them and physically touch her.

For the rest of the card game, Abby kept her attention on the cards and averted from Mac. She couldn't concentrate on the game with his wicked eyes flirting with her.

By the time they finished playing it was nearing midnight and Mac insisted they must go home. Charley walked with Lauren out to the car while Mac lingered with Abby at the door. "Thank you for a wonderful evening," he said, moving to stand just in front of her.

"Don't thank me. I enjoyed it," Abby replied, self-consciously wetting her lips with the tip of her tongue. She hadn't meant it as an open invitation for him to taste her mouth, but he must have taken it as such. Before she could say another word his lips moved to capture hers.

"Hmm, I've wanted to do that all evening," he murmured, slowly drawing back from her and gazing at her face. "I know you said the other night that we needed to go slowly. Would it be hurrying things too much if I asked to see you again tomorrow night?"

"I'd like that," Abby answered shyly, surprised at the depth of her own desire to be with him, to spend more time in his company.

"Good. I'll call you tomorrow." He released her, and with a smile, he left. Abby leaned against the doorjamb, watching him walk away, a smile lingering on her lips.

Minutes later Abby and Charley cleaned up the kitchen. "It was fun tonight, wasn't it, Mom," Charley said as she put the cards back in their box.

"Yes, it was fun," Abby agreed.

"We beat you guys really bad in that last game," she said, grinning widely.

"Yes, you did," Abby said with a laugh.

Charley sat down at the table and watched as Abby put the last of the glasses and cups in the dishwasher. "When we were all sitting here playing cards, it felt good, sort of like we were a real family." Charley grinned crookedly. "It made me feel all warm inside. Does that sound crazy?"

Abby leaned down and gave her daughter a hug. "No, it doesn't sound crazy at all." In fact, it was exactly the way Abby had felt. And it was a wonderful feeling.

"More popcorn?" Abby asked Mac, passing him the large bowl from the coffee table.

"Thanks." He reached into the bowl, his gaze not wavering from the television screen where an old movie played.

He's as intense watching TV as he is in everything else he does, she thought, and smiled as she popped several fluffy kernels of corn into her mouth.

His arm rested comfortably across her back, his fingers absently caressing her shoulder. His scent surrounded her, a hint of spice that made her snuggle closer, enjoying his nearness. She'd been right when she'd imagined that his body would be perfect for cuddling. It was.

It was difficult to believe that it had only been two weeks since they'd had their first official date. They'd seen each other almost every evening since then. They'd gone to a concert—Mac's desire to change her mind about classical music. She'd made him take her dancing the next night at a club that specialized in old rock and roll music.

But most evenings they'd spent here at Abby's, watching television or playing board games with the girls.

Abby was amazed at how quickly they'd become comfortable with each other, how well their lifestyles melded together. She was also surprised at the passion between them, a passion that was held in check only because of circumstances and timing and the constant company of their daughters.

Tonight the girls were shopping at the mall for a couple of hours while Mac and Abby enjoyed their movie and some time alone together.

"That was great," he declared as the ending credits rolled across the screen. "They don't make movies like they used to."

Abby nodded her agreement. "This one and *Casablanca* are my favorites."

"I love *Casablanca*. We'll have to get a copy and watch it some night."

Abby smiled at him, leaning into the warmth of his body. "At least we finally found something we share a passion for... old classics."

Mac shifted his position on the sofa and grinned, a wicked glow in his eyes. "Oh, I can think of something else we share a passion for," he murmured, his lips sweeping over hers.

"Your Honor, I object," she teased, her heart responding to his kiss by rapidly accelerating its beat.

"Overruled," he growled, his arms wrapping around her and pulling her closer.

He kissed her soundly, thoroughly and, as always, Abby responded with a fervor she'd never known she possessed. She melted against him, enjoying the tactile sensation of her soft breasts pressed tightly against the unyielding strength of his firm chest.

She parted her lips for him, their tongues entwining in their own dance of passion. He gently maneuvered her so that he was lying on top of her, their bodies stretched out the length of the sofa. She moaned as he pressed his body closer, letting her feel the physical evidence of his desire for her.

"Oh, Abby," he murmured, his hands moving up inside her sweatshirt where he deftly pushed up her bra and caressed her bared breasts. His palms rubbed across her erect nipples, and he groaned as he felt them swell beneath his touch. He couldn't ever remember wanting a woman as he wanted her. He rained kisses down her neck, moving lower until his lips touched the sweet fullness of her breast. He paused there, tasting her, needing more, wanting more.

"Do you have any idea how much I want you?" he gasped.

Abby's body screamed with need as desire swirled around her, threatening to overwhelm her. She struggled to maintain her sanity, something niggling in the back of her mind, warning her that the timing wasn't right.

"Abby, let me make love to you."

His words caused a shiver of excitement to tingle up her spine, a tingle that froze as a noise sounded just outside her apartment door.

Abby shoved Mac up and off, and ran for the bathroom, making it inside just as she heard the girls enter the apartment. She straightened her clothing, finger combed her hair and took a couple of deep breaths. She heard Mac greet the girls and Charley explain that they'd gotten a ride home from Mrs. Carver, the woman who lived in the apartment next door. Feeling like she was now under control, Abby left the bathroom.

"Hey, Mom, you should see all the cool stuff we got on sale," Charley greeted her, holding up three bags from three different stores.

"Looks like you bought out the store," Abby said, looking over at Mac, who looked the picture of innocence casually eating popcorn. She sat down at the other end of the sofa, hoping she looked as innocent as he did.

"Did you find anything exciting to spend your allowance on?" Mac asked Lauren.

"I got a few things," she said, not looking at him. "Come on, Charley, let's go into your room." Without waiting for an answer, she disappeared into Charley's room. With a shrug of her shoulders, Charley quickly followed her friend.

"Whew, that was close," Abby whispered the moment they had gone. Mac nodded absently. "And did I sense a little tension between father and daughter?" she asked, moving closer to him on the sofa.

Mac sighed and leaned forward, running a hand through his hair in distraction. "She's been angry with me for the past two days. She doesn't want to take the bus to school anymore. She wants to catch a ride with a bunch of kids who drive and I told her no." He sighed again. "I've been getting the silent treatment since then."

Abby smiled and placed a hand on his arm in sympathy. "If it's any consolation, it's been my experience that most teenagers can't sustain the silent treatment for very long."

"She thinks I'm too strict."

"Are you?" Abby asked.

He looked at her in surprise. "I don't think I am. I'm determined that Lauren will have the right values, that she'll learn the importance of trust. I don't want her to become like her...like so many kids I see in court."

Abby was silent for a moment. She'd known what he'd been about to say, that he didn't want Lauren to be like her mother. "Mac, she's a good kid. She's at an age when a little bit of independence is important. It's what helps teenagers mature and grow."

"She can mature and grow under my watchful eye," Mac answered, and his tone of voice let Abby know the subject was closed.

Later, with Lauren waiting for him in the car. Mac stood at the door bidding good-night to Abby. "I want to finish the discussion we were having before the girls got home," he said, his eyes darkening as he ran a finger down her cheek.

"I don't remember much of a discussion," Abby teased.

"You know what I mean," he growled, leaning down to capture her lips in a soft kiss. He held her for a moment, then reluctantly released her. "It's getting more and more difficult to leave you, Abby

Jones." With these words, he murmured good-night and went out to his car.

It wasn't until much later when Charley was in bed that Abby sat on the sofa and thought about Mac. It was crazy how he had come to complete her life. She hadn't realized there was a void until he'd filled it.

She'd thought she was self-sufficient, content with her life of work and Charley, but now she realized she'd been denying an important part of herself—the feminine side that needed a companion to laugh with, a lover to love.

Two weeks ago she hadn't even been sure she liked Mac Stewart, and now she couldn't imagine what her life would be like if he were to leave it. He'd said it was getting more and more difficult to leave her each night. For her it was getting more and more difficult to let him go.

I'm in love with him. The thought struck her from out of the blue, causing her to catch her breath in shock. Once the initial surprise passed, the thought settled around her like a comfortable quilt on a wintry night. Yes, loving Mac warmed her from the inside out. She loved the way he laughed, not just with his mouth, but with his heart. She adored the way his dark eyebrows drew together when he concentrated. She loved the way his gray eyes darkened just before he kissed her. But more than all of this, she admired his commitment to Lauren and his work, his sense of rightness and his strength of character. He was a good man and she loved him. And she had a feeling that, whether he knew it or not, Mac was falling in love with her, as well.

Humming beneath her breath, Abby gathered up the popcorn bowl and their drink glasses and took them to the kitchen. He'd only been gone a few minutes and already she couldn't wait until tomorrow when she would see him again. "Oh yes, you've got it bad, Abby girl," she said to herself, then laughed out loud with sheer delight.

"I'm sorry, Abby. I forgot all about having night court this evening." Mac's disappointment was obvious over the phone line the next evening.

"It's okay. We'll just see each other tomorrow night. Besides, with you not here I'll have a chance to get some papers graded that I've been putting off."

"I miss you already," Mac said softly. "I was thinking, maybe this weekend we'll tell the girls we're going to a movie or something. We'll let them stay at your place, then you and I will sneak over to my house and have some time alone."

Abby hesitated a moment, knowing exactly what he had in mind. If they went to his place and had no threat of interruptions, she knew they would make love. "That sounds wonderful," she replied, feeling her cheeks flush with warmth. She was ready for their relationship to deepen, trusting in the love that was growing between them.

"Wear that fluffy blue robe this evening while you're grading your papers," he said.

"What?" Abby laughed. "Why?"

"So while I'm working tonight I'll have a vision of you in that robe that perfectly matches the color of your eyes."

"I'll go put it on the minute I hang up."

They said their goodbyes and Abby slowly hung up the phone, shaking her head in wonder. Could this be the same man she'd thought was a stuffy, overbearing cold fish? Mac had transformed himself in the past couple of weeks, showing himself to be a loving, passionate man.

She moved into the bedroom and pulled her robe out of the closet. For a long moment she held the fluffy material in her arms, absently caressing the softness as she thought of what Mac had suggested for the weekend.

It somehow seemed right that they deepen their growing commitment to one another by making love. She loved him, and she desperately wanted to show him just how much. She closed her eyes, for a moment imagining the two of them together, their bodies moving in sync, their breaths quickening with passion. She shivered and quickly undressed, then pulled the robe tightly around her.

She was just about to leave the bedroom when the phone rang once again. "Abby?"

"Hello, Harry. How are the wedding plans coming?" she asked, sitting down on the edge of the bed.

"They're not." Harry's voice was positively miserable. "It's all been called off."

"Oh no. Harry, what happened?"

"Could we get together and talk? Abby, I really need a friend."

"Of course," she answered without hesitation. "Do you want me to come over to your place?"

"I'm not at home. I'm down at the courthouse. You know the coffee shop a block from here?"

"Sure," Abby answered, remembering where she'd eaten with Mac before the camping trip.

"Could you meet me there, say in half an hour?"

"I'll be there."

Minutes later Abby steered her car toward the coffee shop where she was to meet Harry, her mind whirling with questions as she wondered why the wedding plans had been cancelled. The last time she'd spoken with Harry they had been moving along quite smoothly.

As she parked the car, she thought about going into the courtroom and seeing Mac, then dismissed the idea. He'd called her on his dinner break and she didn't want to distract him from his work.

She spied Harry the minute she walked into the coffee shop. He sat alone near the back, looking dejected and bewildered. Abby made her way through the tables to join him, noticing that his face was drawn with unhappiness.

"Harry," she greeted him, leaning down to give him a quick kiss on the cheek. She slid into the seat across from him and took his hands in hers. "What's going on?"

"Women," Harry said disparagingly. "Whatever possessed me to consider giving up my bachelorhood for one of those fickle, crazy creatures?"

"Harry, tell me what happened."

He paused as the waitress appeared at their table. Harry ordered coffee for them both, then looked back at Abby. "It's this wedding thing. It's changed a sweet, soft-spoken, loving woman into a complete shrew. Kathleen has gone crazy. We started out agreeing on a small, intimate ceremony for close friends and relatives. Slowly but surely it's evolved into a bloody circus." As he spoke he methodically shredded his paper napkin into tiny pieces. "All I did was suggest we try to keep things simple and she went nuts, told me I didn't love her, that I was only concerned about the cost of the wedding. Then she told me to just forget the whole damned thing."

"Sounds to me like prewedding jitters," Abby said with a smile. "Probably what Kathleen needs most is reassurance that you love her and you'll have a wonderful life together."

Harry frowned. "She should know that. After all, I did propose to her."

"Harry." Abby reached out and took his hand in hers once again, putting a halt to his compulsive napkin-shredding. "I don't know a prospective bride and groom who don't go through some tension and trouble as they plan their wedding. What you and Kathleen are going through is pretty normal."

"Heaven help me. If this is normal, give me insanity."

Abby laughed. "Where is Kathleen now?"

"At home. I called her a little while ago and she was crying."

"Go over there and take her in your arms and tell her you love her. I guarantee things will work out just fine."

"You really think so?" Hope lighted his pale eyes.

"I know so." She blinked in surprise as Harry jumped up from his chair and pulled a couple of dollars out of his pocket.

"Here, this is for the coffee. I'd better get going before I lose my nerve." He reached out and took Abby's hand and kissed the back of it. "You're a love, Abby, and a good friend. Thanks for the advice."

"Call me and let me know what happens," Abby called after him as he hurried out of the coffee shop. Abby smiled, somehow knowing Harry and Kathleen would be fine.

As she left the coffee shop she once again considered stopping at the courthouse and seeing Mac, then dismissed the idea. He'd been on the bench and probably wouldn't even know she was there. Besides, she'd run out of the house without leaving a note for Charley, who was probably home from the library and wondering where Abby had gone. With this thought in mind, Abby headed home.

Abby waited all the next evening to hear from Mac, but her phone remained mysteriously silent. "Did you see Lauren at school today?" Abby asked Charley as they ate supper that evening.

Charley nodded. "Sure, why?"

"I was sort of expecting her and Mac to come over tonight, but I haven't heard from him." She shrugged her shoulder. "I guess something else came up."

"I guess. Lauren didn't say anything one way or the other," Charley said. "She's been pretty mad at her dad lately. She thinks he treats her like a baby."

"He worries about her," Abby replied, picking unenthusiastically at her baked chicken.

"According to Lauren, he worries too much."

"I'm sure they'll work things out," Abby commented.

Charley looked at her slyly, a small grin lifting her impish mouth. "You and Mac are getting along real well, aren't you?"

"Yes, we are," Abby said, unable to stifle the smile that sprang to her lips.

"You know you have Lauren and me to thank." Charley smiled smugly. "We knew you'd be perfect for each other. All we had to do was get you guys together."

"Charley, relationships are a little more complicated than just throwing two people together and hoping for the best," Abby replied. Impulsively she reached over and gave her daughter a hug. "But I think in this case you were right."

Why hasn't he called? Abby wondered as she got ready for bed that evening. Since their first real date not a day had gone by that they hadn't at least spoken to each other. She hoped he wasn't sick or that nothing was seriously wrong. Surely if that had been the case, Lauren would have said something to Charley.

She couldn't believe how much she had come to anticipate seeing him, or at the very least, hearing his voice. It was amazing that in such a brief period of time he'd become such an important part of her life.

Something must have cropped up that deterred him from calling. *He's a prominent, busy man,* she reminded herself. *I'll hear from him tomorrow,* she thought with pleasure as she drifted off to sleep.

But she didn't. Again the next evening the phone remained ominously silent. Mustering up her courage, she called him, reaching his answering machine and leaving a message. The next morning she again got his machine and left another message. For the first time, she began to wonder if something wasn't horribly wrong.

Chapter Ten

"Charley, I'm home," Abby called tiredly as she entered the apartment.

"I'll be out in a minute," Charley called from behind her closed bedroom door.

Abby flopped down on the sofa and kicked off her shoes. Leaning her head back she released a weary sigh. She'd like to think her tiredness was a product of working late for the past two nights. But in her heart she knew it was more than that. A full week had passed and she hadn't heard a word from Mac. Not only had he not returned her phone messages, the weekend had come and gone without a word from him. It was supposed to be the weekend when they made love, cemented the feelings they had for one another. What could have possibly kept him from calling her?

As much as she wanted to know why he hadn't called, what was going on, her pride wouldn't allow her to make a third phone call to him. And beneath her worry and weariness, she was beginning to feel the stirrings of a healthy dose of self-righteous anger.

She'd thought she and Mac were in the process of building something real, something lasting. So what had prompted the last five days of silence?

"Mom, can I talk to you for a minute?" Charley came out of her bedroom and perched on the edge of the sofa. "First you have to promise me you won't get mad."

"Oh, Charley, I'm much too tired to play games tonight. What do you want to talk about?"

Charley hesitated a moment. "Lauren is in my bedroom. She's run away from home and she doesn't want anyone to know she's here."

Abby stifled a groan. She had a feeling something was already very wrong between her and Mac. She certainly wouldn't improve anything by harboring his fugitive daughter without telling him. "Tell Lauren to come out here. It sounds like we all need to talk."

Charley nodded solemnly and disappeared into her bedroom. She returned moments later with Lauren lagging behind, her face a mask of defiant unhappiness.

"Sit down, girls," Abby instructed, waiting until both of them were settled on the floor in front of her. "What's going on, Lauren?"

"My dad's mean and hateful and I don't want to live with him anymore," she blurted out, her blue eyes misting with the burden of unshed tears.

"What brought on this particular crisis?" Abby asked, rubbing two fingers at her temple where a headache pounded dully.

"The last couple of days I've stayed late after school for some extra help in algebra." Lauren flushed and swiped at an errant tear with the back of her hand. "I'm not very good at math and my grade isn't so great. Dad thinks grades are super important so I thought I could get some extra help before report cards are sent out." She paused a moment and Charley threw an arm around her shoulders in a show of support.

"Anyway," Lauren continued, "Dad came home early today and caught me coming in late from school. He totally freaked out and accused me of being dishonest and sneaking out to meet boys."

"Did you explain to him about staying after school?" Abby asked gently.

Lauren nodded miserably. "But he wouldn't listen. He never listens. He always thinks the worst." Her voice rose as sobs of frustration shook her shoulders. "He's so afraid I'm going to turn out like her."

Abby didn't have to ask who the "her" referred to. She knew it was Lauren's mother, Mac's ex-wife.

"Lauren, you know that staying here isn't going to solve anything between you and your father. You also know I can't let you stay here without your father knowing it. He's probably worried sick about you."

Lauren shot an accusatory glare at Charley. "I told you she'd tell my dad."

Charley looked almost as miserable as Lauren.

"Lauren, you want your father to see that you're becoming an adult. Adults don't run away from problems. They face them." As Abby spoke these words, she realized she needed to take some of her own advice. If there was a problem between her and Mac that she wasn't aware of, then she shouldn't let pride keep her from discussing it with him. Their relationship was much too important.

"I guess you're right," Lauren replied reluctantly.

"Do you want me to call your father or do you want to?"

Lauren grinned. "Would you? I'm trying to be grown up, but I guess I'm not quite there yet."

Abby leaned over and patted Lauren's arm. "I'm sure everything will work out just fine," she assured her. "Why don't you two go on back into the bedroom and I'll call Mac."

The girls ran for the bedroom as if it was a safe haven. When they had gone, Abby reached for the phone. She hoped that Mac's silence of the past several days was a result of his problems with Lauren. Abby well knew how problems with children could throw your entire life off track. She quickly dialed his number. He answered on the first ring, his voice tense.

"Mac, it's Abby. Lauren is here."

"I'll be right over," he responded brusquely, disconnecting before Abby had a chance to say anything more.

True to his words, within minutes a loud pounding on the door announced his arrival. Abby opened the door, for a moment merely drinking in his presence.

"Where is she?" he asked, pushing past her into the apartment.

"In the bedroom. But before you talk to her, can we talk?"

For a moment he looked as if the very idea was physically painful, then his features regained their initial coldness. "What do we have to talk about?"

Abby looked at him incredulously. "Mac, it's me, Abby. What's going on? Didn't you get my messages? Why haven't you called me?"

"I've been busy."

"Too busy for a single phone call?" She eyed him in disbelief. He was in his judge mode, his face all hard lines and his expression closed. Abby felt his distance but she didn't know what caused it or how to breach it. "Mac, Lauren explained to me what happened, about her staying after school for math help," Abby said, deciding to deal with the situation at hand. Maybe the problems with Lauren had him withdrawing and acting so strangely.

"She sneaked around behind my back instead of being open and up front with me. She knows I can't abide deception." His gaze focused intently on Abby. "I'll tolerate a lot of things, but never deception."

Abby had the distinct impression that he wasn't talking just about the problems with Lauren. *He can't be talking about me,* she thought, her conscience clear. "Lauren knows it was wrong of her not to tell you she was staying after school, but don't you think you're overreacting a bit to a simple misunderstanding?"

"I don't expect you to understand," he snapped.

"What's that supposed to mean?" Abby asked, the threat of anger welling up in her throat. What was wrong with him? Why was he acting this way?

"It means, why should I expect you to understand the importance of trust when you tell me one thing and you do another?" Gone was his aura of control. His face twisted in anger and beneath the sparks of rage in his smoky eyes she saw something else—hurt.

She wanted to take him into her arms, stroke away the angry wrinkles in his brow. She stifled this impulse and instead reached out and touched his arm.

"Mac, what are you talking about?" she asked in confusion.

He shrugged off her hand as if it was merely an annoyance. "I'm talking about last Wednesday night, when we spoke on the phone and you told me you'd be here all night grading papers." His mouth was a grim, tight line and he looked like a stranger... an angry stranger.

"What about it?" Abby asked impatiently.

"We had a brief recess in court and I went down to the coffee shop. Guess what I saw? You and some man holding hands across the table."

Abby stared at him incredulously. "That's what this is all about? That's why you haven't called? Because of some misguided jealousy?"

"This has nothing to do with jealousy. It's about trust," Mac snapped, his last bit of control gone as he stomped cross the room, then turned back to look at her. "You told me you were staying at home. When I saw you there in the coffee shop I felt like I'd been kicked in the stomach. It was just like before," he broke off with a flush and drew a deep breath. "You lied to me."

"I didn't lie," Abby retorted angrily. "I had planned on staying home all night. Then I got a phone call from a friend who needed some emotional support. I didn't realize I was supposed to check with you before making other plans." She glared back at him, the pain and anger of the last five days boiling to the surface. "You're doing the same thing to me that you are to Lauren, misconstruing a simple situation. What's worse is that you didn't give me the benefit of the doubt. You didn't give me a chance to explain. You found me guilty and sentenced me before giving me a trial."

Her anger passed as quickly as it had surfaced and instead her heart filled with a dreadful heaviness. She sank onto the sofa, her legs feeling like lead weights as a horrid resignation suffused her. "Weeks ago you told me that you thought you were ready to close one chapter of your life and move on to a new one. You're wrong, Mac. You can't move on. You're frozen in time, weighed down by too much emotional baggage left over from your marriage."

"What are you talking about?" he scoffed, his voice still laced with anger.

Abby gazed up at him, loving him, wishing she could crawl inside him, touch the wounds existing there and magically heal them. But she knew it was impossible. "Oh, Mac, your ex-wife hurt you, and you're blaming Lauren and me for all her mistakes. You're punishing us for her betrayal. She not only divorced you, she crippled you emotionally. Until you deal with this issue, there's no hope of your getting on with your life."

"Lauren!" Mac bellowed, then looked at Abby. "You don't know what you're talking about and I'm not going to stand here and listen to you dissect me." He stopped speaking as Lauren entered the room. "Go get in the car," he instructed her. Abby watched as Lauren shot her a look of pure misery, then disappeared out the door. "And I'll thank you to leave the raising of my daughter to me," he added.

Abby stood up and moved closer to him, needing to connect, wanting to get past this wide chasm that yawned between them. She made one final appeal. "Mac, when you're sitting on the bench, I've seen you give defendants a second chance, but with us, the people who love you, you show no mercy."

"The people who love me shouldn't need any mercy," he replied coolly, then disappeared out the door.

For a long moment after he had gone, Abby stood rooted to the floor in the living room, unable to believe what had just happened. She stared at the door he'd shut with such finality.

It was crazy... all because she'd decided to go to Harry when he'd needed someone to talk to. And yet she knew instinctively that if it had not been Harry, it would have been a similar situation that would have provoked the same argument. She'd been right. Mac was emotionally crippled. He talked of trust, but had none to give. His wife had stolen more from him than a marriage. Until he healed these old wounds, he couldn't move on to a healthy, loving relationship. And she wouldn't make a life with a man who was so emotionally stunted.

She slowly sank back onto the sofa, her heart aching with the realization of her loss. He was gone... really gone from her life. If only it were as easy to banish him from her heart.

Mac was angry, angrier than he could ever remember being in his life. For the next three days the anger ate at him, like a festering wound that wouldn't heal.

He knew he was being a bear both at home and at work. He'd overheard two lawyers speculating on the cause of his foul mood, and at home Lauren was once again giving him the silent treatment.

At night when he was too tired to sustain the anger that propelled him boldly through each day, he found himself thinking about what Abby had said to him. Over and over again her words replayed, haunting him, hurting him.

When he'd walked into the coffee shop last week and saw her there, it had been like a bad memory resurfacing from his past. Melinda had often told him she was doing one thing, then sneaked behind his back to do another. Seeing Abby there in the shop had not only been a kick in his stomach, it had also been a spear straight through his heart.

And beneath all the pain, beneath the betrayal, he missed her. Her absence was a constant ache, a void in his soul. In the past couple of weeks he'd begun to fantasize a future with her, a lifetime of days of laughter and nights of loving. Now it was all shattered, lying in pieces at his feet.

Saturday morning he awoke after another restless night. It was his day off and the hours stretched empty before him. *I should go see Melinda.* The thought struck him out of the blue, causing him to choke on his orange juice. He set the glass down and walked over to the window. He stared out blankly, contemplating, dreading what he realized he must do.

It took him three phone calls to get Melinda's address. Although she occasionally called to speak to Lauren, Mac had neither seen nor spoken to her since the day she'd walked out on him. Even their divorce had been handled by intermediaries.

Was it possible Abby had been right? Was it possible he had some unfinished business with Melinda? He stared down at the piece of paper where he had written her address. It suddenly seemed important that he find out.

An hour later Mac sat in his car staring at the house where Melinda lived. It was a small house, neat and tidy on the outside, with leaves from its nearby trees raked into a large pile on the lawn. The remains of a flower bed, now awaiting the arrival of winter, edged the cracked sidewalk that led up to the front door.

Strange, he'd expected something bigger, more ostentatious. He'd always assumed Melinda had left him to move onward and upward.

He remained in the car, dreading the thought of facing her once again. What if he discovered he still loved her? Even as he thought of the possibility, he dismissed it when a vision of Abby filled his mind. He could see Abby's mouth curved up in a generous smile, her blue eyes sparkling with laughter. He remembered the taste of her, the way she moaned deep in her throat whenever he kissed her. No, he didn't have to worry about still being in love with Melinda. How could he love her when his heart belonged to another?

He got out of his car and approached the front door. He didn't want to do this, but he had a feeling it was something that must be done... for himself... for Abby.

Straightening his shoulders he knocked.

"Mac." Her face registered her surprise when she opened the door.

For a moment he simply looked at her, waiting for something... anger, bitterness, some emotion. But there was none. It was like facing an old acquaintance, a person who had once meant something, but who belonged to another lifetime. "Hello, Melinda."

"What are you doing here? Is Lauren...?" Fear splashed across her delicate features.

"Lauren is just fine," he quickly assured her. "Could I come in? I need to talk to you."

She hesitated a moment, then slowly opened the door for him. Mac drew a steadying breath as he went in to face his demons.

* * *

Abby was getting ready for bed when she heard strange noises coming from Charley's bedroom. She paused outside her daughter's door and listened. Charley was crying.

Abby knocked softly and opened the door. "Charley, are you all right?"

"I'm fine." Charley's voice was muffled by the pillow, where she buried her face.

"Do you always cry when you're fine?" Abby sat down on the edge of the bed. She turned on the bedside lamp and placed a hand on Charley's slender back. "You want to talk about it?" Charley shrugged her shoulders and a muffled sob escaped. "Are you having problems at school?" Abby inquired, her heart squeezing at the sound of her daughter's unhappiness. She could stand anything, but she couldn't deal with the knowledge that Charley was unhappy.

Charley's head nodded negatively. "School is fine," she choked.

"Then, honey, what is it?"

"It's you," Charley blurted, her shoulders shaking with uncontrollable sobs.

"Me? Are we having a fight I don't know about?" Abby patted Charley's back. "Turn over and talk to me, Charley."

Reluctantly Charley rolled over and peered at Abby with tear-swollen eyes. "Now, what's this all about?" Abby asked.

"You... and Mac," Charley answered.

Abby's heart lurched painfully at the sound of his name. "What about us?" Abby asked, carefully keeping her voice devoid of pain.

Charley threw herself into Abby's arms, her slim body shaking. "It's all my fault," the girl sobbed. "Lauren and me... we should never have played matchmakers. It's all my fault that you have a broken heart." Charley dissolved into sobs.

"Oh, honey." Abby hugged her daughter close, feeling an answering glimmer of tears pressing at her own eyes. She'd thought she'd been functioning very well since the night Mac had stormed out of her life. She'd thought she'd hidden her devastation, her heartache very well. It had only been late at night, when she was alone in her bed with her thoughts that she'd allowed her strength to ebb and the tears to flow. But apparently, Charley was more highly attuned to her pain than she'd imagined.

"Charley, none of this is your fault. Mac and I had problems that were adult problems. They had absolutely nothing to do with you and Lauren."

"But everything was going along so great. Lauren and I thought we'd get to be sisters, that we'd all be a family. Oh, Mom, it hurts so much."

Abby realized then that not only was Charley crying for Abby's pain, but Charley was experiencing a loss herself, grieving for a family she'd imagined she'd have. She held Charley close, feeling her own grief rising to the surface. "We'll be all right, Charley," she consoled, fighting to keep her own tears under control. "We'll get through all this." But her words sounded empty even to herself.

Chapter Eleven

"Charley, I'm home." Abby walked into the apartment and dropped her stack of books onto the table just inside the door. The silence in the apartment echoed hollowly. She sank onto the sofa, rubbing eyes that felt grainy and swollen. She and Charley had been up far too late the night before, holding each other and grieving over what might have been. But all the talking and hugging and crying hadn't eased the despair that made Abby's heart heavy.

"Charley?" she called again, this time loudly. She'd promised Charley that they'd do something fun this evening, something that would take their minds off their heartache.

She pulled herself up from the sofa and walked to Charley's bedroom door and knocked. There was no answer. Abby pushed open the door and looked around, her heart dropping to her feet as she saw the open closet door and the empty interior.

With her heart thudding painfully fast, Abby noticed Charley's suitcase was also missing. What on earth is going on? she wondered, spying a note on the pillow of the bed. She unfolded it with trembling hands.

Mom,
I'm so sorry. I know your heart hurts and it's all my fault. I'm leaving because I can't stand to see you so hurt.
 I love you.
Charlene Renee Jones

Abby threw the note onto the bed, angry with Charley, but more angry with herself. She should have realized last night how deeply troubled Charley was. She should have done something more than just give her a hug and a handful of empty promises about things being all right. She should have come home right after school today instead of working so late.

She walked over to the living-room window and stared out, aware that darkness would be falling soon. She had to find Charley. She couldn't stand the thought of her daughter out on the streets in the dark.

Think, she instructed herself. Where would Charley go? Lauren's, of course. Abby raced to the phone and quickly dialed Mac's number. Her heart did an additional nosedive when she heard Mac's deep voice. "Mac, is Charley over there?"

"No. I was just about to call you to see if Lauren was there."

"So she's gone, too?" Abby's despair grew.

"She left me a note. The two of them must be together somewhere. I'll come over and we'll go looking for them."

Before she could protest, he disconnected. She paced back and forth, her emotions churning. Worry about Charley mingled with the dread of seeing Mac. If she had to live her life without him, then she didn't want to see him again.

But she knew he was right. The girls were probably together and it seemed only right that she and Mac look for them together. In this case two heads were definitely better than one.

She steeled herself when she heard Mac's distinctive knock on the door. How painful it would be to pretend she no longer cared for him. How difficult it would be to look at him and not let him see her love. But that's the way it had to be. She refused to give her heart to half a man. Besides, she had more to worry about, like the whereabouts of her daughter. Where on earth could Charley have gone?

"Hello, Mac," she said as she opened the door to him, pleased to hear that she sounded controlled and businesslike.

"Are you ready to go?" he asked tersely. "I made a mental list of all the places to look for them while I was driving over here."

"Fine, let's go."

This is going to be easy, Abby thought as they drove first toward the library. Mac was distracted, obviously concerned about Lauren. Abby focused on her own worry, shoving any other unwanted emotion aside.

"I know a bunch of the kids meet at the library each night and hang out and do homework together," he explained as he pulled into the Baldwin Municipal Library parking lot.

"Yes, Charley often comes down here for the evening," Abby answered. Together they got out of the car and headed inside. There were plenty of kids there, but not the two they were searching for.

"I'm going to kill her," Abby threatened as they got back into the car and drove to the Pizza Palace, the second location on Mac's mental list. "If this is some kind of a game the two of them are playing, I'm really going to kill her."

"Lauren's in for the same fate," Mac replied, his grip tense on the steering wheel. "Don't they realize what could happen to two girls alone on the streets after dark?"

"Oh, Mac, don't say that," Abby begged, worry forming a hard knot in the pit of her stomach. The worry intensified as they hunted for the girls at the Pizza Palace, the skating rink and in the city park. None of the girls' friends they encountered had seen either girl all evening.

They reached the end of Mac's mental list and sat in the parking lot of the city park, neither knowing where to go from here. Abby stared out the car window, concern now beginning to turn into fear. In the light of the moon she could see the park swings gently swaying to and fro in the night breeze. She'd often brought Charley here as a toddler. Charley loved to swing.

"Mac, where can they be?" she asked, fighting to hold back her tears.

For the first time, her distress communicated itself to him. He turned to her, his arms automatically reaching for her.

Without thought, Abby went into his arms, needing his embrace to warm her, his strength to buoy her. She didn't care what had passed between them before. She forgot the harsh words that had been exchanged. She only knew she needed him now to hold her. "I'm so scared," she whispered into the front of his shirt. "It's getting so late. I don't even know if Charley thought to wear a jacket and it's getting so cold."

"They're smart girls, very resourceful. I'm sure we'll find them and everything will be fine." His hand moved up and caressed her hair, the gesture causing an ache to mingle with her worry.

"Everything isn't fine, and I don't think it ever will be again." Abby moved out of his arms, hating herself for her weakness where he was concerned. They'd find the girls and then she'd never see him again. That was the way it had to be.

"Abby..." He reached out and softly touched her cheek.

She pulled farther back, unable to stand his touch. It wasn't fair what his touch did to her, the way it made her insides warm and her thinking cloudy. She had to maintain control. She drew a deep breath. "I'm sorry. Let's go find the girls."

"I think we need to talk first," Mac said, shutting off the engine and unbuckling his seat belt so he could fully face her. "I went to see Melinda this morning."

Abby stared at him. Of all the things she'd expected him to say, this wasn't one of them. "Oh?" She didn't know what else to add.

"You were absolutely right when you told me I had some unfinished business with her." He paused a moment, then continued, "I couldn't believe the way I felt when she opened the door and I saw her."

"Oh," Abby repeated, dread crawling up her throat as she saw a look of gratitude on his face. He still loved Melinda. *That's what he's going to tell me, that he looked at his ex-wife and realized he was still in love with her,* Abby thought miserably. *If he thanks me for getting them back together, I'll lose it and blubber like a baby.*

"Abby, it was so strange. She opened the door and I looked at her for a long moment and I waited, but nothing happened. I felt nothing...nothing at all. It was like meeting with a stranger." He reached out once again and touched her face, and this time Abby didn't, couldn't draw away from his caress. "And the worst thing of all was that all I could think of was the things you said to me."

"I...I had no right to say those things to you," Abby replied softly. "It wasn't my place."

"If the woman I love doesn't have the right to tell me some hard truths, then who does?"

"Oh, Mac, don't make this harder than it already is," Abby answered, her eyes filling with tears. What good did it do for her to be the woman he loved? She couldn't live with his mistrust. She couldn't love him never knowing what little misunderstanding would make him withdraw, grow cold.

"Let me finish." His hand moved across her cheek to capture a teardrop that fell from her eye. "You were right when you told me I was punishing you and Lauren for Melinda's mistakes. The sad thing is for the past three years I've been blaming her for a lot of my own mistakes."

"What... what do you mean?" Abby looked at him, puzzled.

Mac released his hold on her and ran a hand through his hair, staring unseeing out the car window. "When Melinda left me, it was easy to lay blame at her doorstep, to feel betrayed and bitter. It was much easier to do all that than to face my own shortcomings and accept part of the responsibility for the demise of the marriage." He sighed heavily, a look of pain in his eyes as he gazed at her once again.

"Melinda and I talked, really talked today about our marriage, and as we did I realized we both failed each other. I was so caught up in my work, trying to make a name for myself and be the best judge I could be, that I forgot about being a husband. I neglected her, expecting her to be happy in the shadows while I reached for the moon. She tried many times to tell me we were losing touch with each other, but I was too busy to listen." He looked back out the car window. "You made me so angry the other night. And this morning I realized I've been angry for three years. You were right. I've been taking out my anger and fears on Lauren and you. I was so afraid of being hurt again." He sighed and turned to smile at her. "I had planned on calling you this evening, before the girls pulled this stunt."

"I...I don't know what to say," Abby said truthfully, unsure what he expected from her.

"Say you'll marry me." He gazed at her and this time she saw no shadows of his past, no anger, no lingering pain reflected there. She saw only love, strong and true.

"Oh, Mac," she breathed, unable to believe her ears.

He pulled her back into his arms. "Tell me you'll marry me, Abby Jones. Promise you'll keep me from becoming stuffy, bitter Stoneface."

"Yes, yes, I'll marry you." Abby laughed, the vise that had been a band of pain around her heart releasing its grip. "On one condition," she added warningly. "I will not be a neglected wife."

"That's a condition I'll gladly comply with," he agreed, his mouth finding hers in a kiss that held all the promise, all the passion of their love.

"Mac...the girls," she reminded him, reluctantly pulling away from him. As much as she'd love to go on kissing him forever, as happy as she was at the moment, her joy was tempered with worry.

"What girls?" he answered, then smiled and released her. "Okay, let's go find the little stinkers, then we'll continue where we left off."

"You've got a date," Abby replied, her heart swollen with emotion as she gazed at him.

They drove around for another half hour with no success, and finally decided to go back to Abby's and wait for word from the two runaways. "Lauren won't be happy with the consequences when I finally get hold of her," Mac promised as he pulled up in front of Abby's apartment building.

"Mac, look." Abby pointed to the stairs that led up to the front door. Mac's headlights played on two figures sitting there, suitcases on either side of them. "Thank God," Abby breathed in relief just before anger overtook her. Together she and Mac got out of the car and approached the girls.

"Get inside, both of you," Mac said, his voice stern as he glared at them.

The two girls looked at each other, then scurried to comply with his demand. "Leave this to me," Mac whispered to Abby as they followed the girls into Abby's apartment. When they were all inside, he pointed to the sofa. "Both of you sit there." When they were seated, he walked over and placed an arm around Abby's shoulders. "Do you two have any idea how worried we've been about you? Do you have any idea what kinds of things can happen to two girls alone after dark?"

Charley and Lauren looked miserable. "We just wanted to give you guys one more chance," Lauren said, her eyes not quite meeting her father's critical gaze.

"Yeah, you're both so miserable apart," Charley added, she, too, having problems meeting her mother's eyes.

"We had to think of a way to get you guys back together and we couldn't think of any other way," Lauren explained. "We figured if we both ran away, you two would get together to look for us."

"Anyway, it looks like it worked," Charley ventured, a little smile on her face.

"What worked is that you've both managed to get yourselves grounded," Mac replied.

Both girls moaned. "For how long?" Lauren asked.

"At least until after the wedding, maybe longer," Mac returned.

"Oh, Dad," Lauren moaned, then stopped as his words penetrated. "A wedding? You guys are getting married?"

Abby nodded, laughing as the two girls jumped off the sofa and hugged each other.

"We're going to be sisters! We're going to be sisters!" they chanted in unison.

"Grounded sisters," Mac exclaimed, his arm tightening around Abby.

"We don't care," Charley exclaimed. "We're all going to be married and live happily ever after."

"Sounds like a life sentence to me," Mac said, smiling at Abby.

"And, Your Honor, I have absolutely no objections," Abby replied, raising her lips to meet his.

Epilogue

Abby stared at her reflection in the full-length mirror. The wedding dress fit her to perfection, hugging her slender shape and falling in graceful lines to the floor. Her heart beat so rapidly she imagined she could see it pounding through the heavily beaded bodice of the gown.

She looked at her wristwatch and shivered in anticipation. In exactly five minutes she would walk down the church aisle and become Mrs. Mac Stewart.

It had been exactly one month since the night the girls had run away and Mac had proposed. The time since then had flown by on wings of love and laughter as they'd planned their wedding and their future together.

Mac had made great strides in healing the wounds of his past. He'd even been instrumental in setting up weekly visits between Melinda and Lauren. Lauren insisted on choosing to remain with her dad. And after the wedding the four of them would live together in Mac's home. Abby was pleased that the girl seemed to be making peace with her mother.

And tonight Mac and I will finally have our night alone, Abby thought, smiling. At last they would get the opportunity to explore the depths of their passion and indulge their desire for each other.

A knock sounded on the door. "Mom?" Abby turned as Charley and Lauren entered the room. "Oh, Mom, you look so beautiful," Charley exclaimed.

"Like a fairy princess," Lauren added.

"You two look pretty terrific yourselves," Abby replied. As Abby's bridesmaids, they looked like dolls in matching pale blue dresses. "Just like real sisters."

They smiled widely at each other. "I can't believe this is all really coming true," Charley chirped happily. "This is like the very best dream in the whole world really happening." She threw her arm around Lauren, who nodded and grinned in agreement.

"You two just remember. You both promised us no more schemes, no more of your crazy manipulations," Abby reminded them. They nodded soberly. Abby gave them each a nervous hug.

"Abby, it's time," somebody yelled through the door.

There was a flurry of activity and suddenly Abby found herself standing at the back of the church, nervous butterflies skipping and dancing in the pit of her stomach. She felt a sudden moment of panic. What was she doing here? Mac liked classical music; she liked rock and roll. He loved the fall; she adored the summer. They had absolutely nothing in common. This was crazy!

Her gaze flew down the aisle and she saw Mac, so strong and handsome in his gray tux. His eyes captured hers and a smile curved his lips. Instantly her panic fled as she remembered exactly what it was they had in common. He loved her and she loved him, and that was what was important. Smiling radiantly, she moved down the aisle, her footsteps sure and steady as she walked toward her future.

"Wasn't the wedding awesome?" Charley whispered in the darkness of the bedroom.

"Yeah, your mom looked beautiful," Lauren replied. The two girls were in twin beds in Charley's Aunt Becky's home. They would be staying with Becky for the duration of Mac and Abby's honeymoon.

"Just think, when Mom and Mac get home we're finally ungrounded," Charley reminded her new sister.

"It wasn't so bad being grounded this time." Lauren leaned up on her elbow and gazed at Charley. "I mean, it was all worth it, wasn't it?"

"Sure," Charley agreed. "I wouldn't mind being grounded a whole year if the end result was Mom and Mac getting married and you and me becoming sisters."

"Charley?"

"What?"

"I've been thinking," Lauren said slowly. "Wouldn't it be nice if we had a new brother or sister?"

Charley sat up and stared across the darkened room, seeing Lauren's grin illuminated by the glow of the room's night-light. "What are you talking about?"

Lauren giggled. "You know, a baby. Wouldn't it be great if your mom had a baby?"

"Sure, but how are we gonna accomplish that?" Charley asked curiously.

Lauren got up and pushed her bed against Charley's. "You remember when your mom and my dad made us promise no more schemes or plans?" Charley nodded. "I had my fingers crossed," Lauren said with a giggle. She jumped up on the bed, moved closer to Charley, and whispered, "I've got a great plan...."

* * * * *

4 FREE SILHOUETTE ROMANCE NOVELS AND A FREE GIFT!

Let us spoil you with 4 Silhouette Romance novels plus a beautiful Gold Toned Chain FREE!

. Then, if you choose, go on to enjoy 4 of these sweet Silhouette Romance novels every month for just *$4.24 each – postage and handling FREE! There's no obligation. You can cancel or suspend your subscription at any time.

It's so easy. Send no money now. Simply fill in the coupon below and send it to

Harlequin Mills & Boon Reader Service
Reply Paid 56
Locked Bag 2 Chatswood 2067
NO STAMP REQUIRED

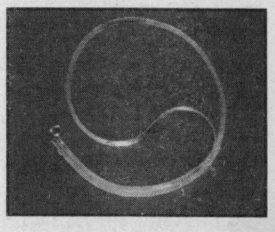

------------------------------------->8---

Yes! Please rush me my 4 free Silhouette Romance novels and **FREE** Gold-Toned Chain! Please also reserve me a Reader Service subscription. If I decide to subscribe I can look forward to receiving 4 Silhouette Romance novels each month for $4.24 each – postage and handling FREE!

If I choose not to subscribe I shall write to you within 10 days – I can keep the books and gift whatever I decide. I can cancel or suspend my subscription at any time. I am over 18 years of age.

SZ 5JGC

Name Mrs/Miss/Ms/Mr _____
PLEASE PRINT

Address _____

Postcode_____ Signature _____

The right is reserved to refuse an application and change the terms of this offer. Offer expires 28th February 1995. Offer available in Australia & New Zealand only.
NZ Price **$5.90** (incl. GST) Postage and Handling FREE
NZ Address: **Harlequin Mills & Boon** FREEPOST 3805, Private Bag 92122, Auckland 1020

SILHOUETTE

Next from Silhouette

SILHOUETTE SPECIAL EDITION

Babies on Board
by Gina Ferris

A is for Always
by Lisa Jackson

Bachelor Dad
by Carole Halston

An Interrupted Marriage
by Laurie Bright

Hesitant Hero
by Christina Dair

High Country Cowboy
by Sandra Moore

SILHOUETTE JASMINE

Simple Gifts
by Kathleen Korbel

Flynn
by Linda Turner

Knight's Corner
by Sibylle Garrett

Jake's Touch
by Mary Anne Wilson

Hero Under Cover
by Suzanne Brockmann

A Piece of Tomorrow
by Kate Stevenson

SILHOUETTE DESIRE

Bewitched
by Jennifer Greene

I'm Gonna Get You
by Lass Small

Mystery Lady
by Jackie Merritt

The Brainy Beauty
by Suzanne Simms

Rafferty's Angel
by Caroline Cross

Stealing Savannah
by Donna Carlisle

SILHOUETTE ROMANCE

The Bachelor Cure
by Pepper Adams

Romancing Cody
by Rena McKay

The Lady Wore Spurs
by Carol Grace

The Wife Next Door
by Carolyn Zane

SILHOUETTE TEMPTATION

Heartstruck
by Elise Title

A Kiss In The Dark
by Tiffany White

Lady Of The Night
by Kate Hoffman

The Bounty Hunter
by Vicki Lewis Thompson

SILHOUETTE INTRIGUE

Midnight Kiss
by Rebecca York

Lost Innocence
by Tina Vasilos

Timewalker
by Aimee Thurlo

Stolen Memories
by Kelsey Roberts

AVAILABLE WHERE GOOD BOOKS ARE SOLD

or contact

harlequin mills & boon reader service
AUSTRALIA: 3 Gibbes Street, Chatswood, NSW 2067.
NEW ZEALAND: Private Bag 92122, Auckland 1020.

SILHOUETTE
Special Edition

SPECIAL 6 EDITION

Very Special Romances This Month

The Parson's Waiting
SHERRYL WOODS

A Home For The Hunter
CHRISTINE RIMMER

Rancher's Heaven
ROBIN ELLIOTT

A River To Cross
LAURIE PAIGE

Miracle Child
KAYLA DANIELS

Family Connections
JUDITH YATES

Available where good books are sold or contact:
HARLEQUIN MILLS & BOON READER SERVICE
Australia: 3 Gibbes Street, Chatswood NSW 2067
New Zealand: Private Bag 92122, Auckland 1020

SILHOUETTE
Special Edition

SPECIAL 6 EDITION

Very Special Romances This Month

The Parson's Waiting
SHERRYL WOODS

A Home For The Hunter
CHRISTINE RIMMER

Rancher's Heaven
ROBIN ELLIOTT

A River To Cross
LAURIE PAIGE

Miracle Child
KAYLA DANIELS

Family Connections
JUDITH YATES

Available where good books are sold or contact:
HARLEQUIN MILLS & BOON READER SERVICE
Australia: 3 Gibbes Street, Chatswood NSW 2067
New Zealand: Private Bag 92122, Auckland 1020

AVAILABLE NOW

SILHOUETTE *Desire*

WRANGLERS LADY
by JACKIE MERRITT

THE COWBOY TAKES A WIFE
by JOAN JOHNSTON

THE DADDY DUE DATE
by RAYE MORGAN

THE HAND OF AN ANGEL
by B. J. JAMES

CAROLINA ON MY MIND
by ANNE MARIE WINSTON

MIDNIGHT ICE
by CATHIE LINZ

Available where good books are sold
or contact:
HARLEQUIN MILLS & BOON READER SERVICE
Australia: 3 Gibbes Street, Chatswood NSW 2067
New Zealand: Private Bag 92122, Auckland 1020

SILHOUETTE
JASMINE

6 great books now available

MICHAELS FATHER
Dallas Schulze

POINT OF NO RETURN
Rachel Lee

WHERE THERE'S SMOKE
Doreen Roberts

MIRANDA'S VIKING
Maggie Shayne

SUSPECT
Jo Leigh

TRUE BLUE
Ingred Weaver

Available where good books are sold or contact:
HARLEQUIN MILLS & BOON READER SERVICE
Australia: 3 Gibbes Street, Chatswood NSW 2067
New Zealand: Private Bag 92122, Auckland 1020

PARTY WORDSEARCH COMPETITION
YOU COULD WIN A YEAR'S SUPPLY OF ROMANCE FICTION FREE!

How would you like a year's supply of Harlequin Mills & Boon romance novels ABSOLUTELY FREE? Well, you can win them! All you have to do is complete the word puzzle below and send it to us by 15th April, 1995. The first 5 correct entries picked out of the barrel after that date will win a year's supply of Harlequin Mills & Boon Romances (10 books every month) FREE. The novels are valued at over £500. What could be easier? Post your entry TODAY!

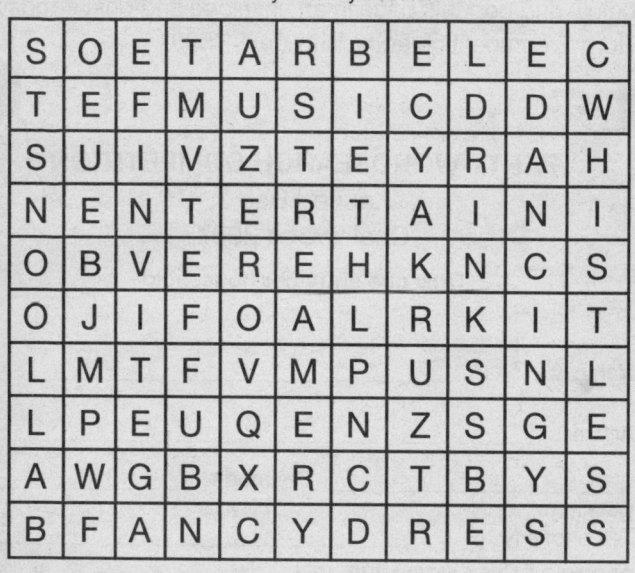

S	O	E	T	A	R	B	E	L	E	C
T	E	F	M	U	S	I	C	D	D	W
S	U	I	V	Z	T	E	Y	R	A	H
N	E	N	T	E	R	T	A	I	N	I
O	B	V	E	R	E	H	K	N	C	S
O	J	I	F	O	A	L	R	K	I	T
L	M	T	F	V	M	P	U	S	N	L
L	P	E	U	Q	E	N	Z	S	G	E
A	W	G	B	X	R	C	T	B	Y	S
B	F	A	N	C	Y	D	R	E	S	S

BALLOONS
DRINKS
ENTERTAIN
BUFFET
CELEBRATE
INVITE

STREAMER
MUSIC
FANCY DRESS
DANCING
PARTIES
WHISTLES

PLEASE TURN OVER FOR DETAILS OF HOW TO ENTER ▶

HOW TO ENTER

The twelve words listed overleaf, below the word puzzle, are hidden in the grid. You can find them by reading the letters backwards and forwards, up, down, and diagonally. As you find each word in the grid put a line through it. When you have completed the wordsearch, fill your name and address details in the space provided below and pop this page in an envelope and post it today. Hurry – competition ends 15th April, 1995.

PARTY WORDSEARCH COMPETITION
*Locked Bag 2,
Chatswood 2067

Only one entry per household

Name (Mrs, Miss, Ms) _____
PLEASE PRINT

Address _____

_____ Postcode _____

Daytime
Telephone No ( ) _____

CLOSING DATE – 15TH APRIL 1995 P1094

*New Zealand Address: Private Bag 92122, Auckland 1020

PLEASE TICK THE BOX IF YOU ARE A SUBSCRIBER. ☐

Competition is open to residents of Australia and New Zealand only. Harlequin Mills and Boon Reader Service is located at 3 Gibbes Street, Chatswood 2067. You may be sent promotional mailings as a result of this entry.